ROYALLY SCHOOLED

MCKENNA JAMES

COPYRIGHT© 2019 Royally Schooled by Mckenna James

Chapter 1

Maggie

The first sip of my coffee nearly scalded me. My tongue stung right before I felt it go numb. Great. I definitely wouldn't be tasting anything today.

Normally I'd be a little more conscious about drinking my coffee at the right temperature, but today I was in a rush. I was already late to an interview for a job I absolutely needed, and I couldn't afford to blow it. So, naturally, my alarm didn't go off on time this morning, and I had just enough time to run a comb through my hair and get dressed before I had to leave.

I was prepared and determined to get this job. I might have looked a mess, and actually be one, but as soon as I walked into that interview, I was going to be cool, calm, and collected. Surely the interview process wouldn't be that rigorous anyway.

An acquaintance had told me of a private job

opening for tutoring two children and thought I might be a good candidate. I couldn't imagine that any parent who would be interviewing me would be too harsh. It wasn't like this was for a serious, stuffy corporate position.

I wanted to look prepared. The quicker I could impress them, the better. This gig paid really well. Every month I struggled to make ends meet and I really needed the money. This job would be minimal hours and high in pay, so I couldn't imagine any situation more perfect for me.

I approached the elegant London hotel where the interview was going to be held. At first, I hadn't questioned meeting at a hotel. There were many prestigious families in London, and I understood they wouldn't want to invite strangers into their home until they had been vetted, and clearly whoever these parents were, they were obviously well-off.

I was, however, genuinely surprised by how fancy it seemed. The entrance to the lobby had these gorgeous white French doors with exquisite gold handles. Apparently, they were even richer than I first imagined. Surely renting out a conference room here wouldn't be cheap, even if it was only for an hour.

With my coffee in one hand along with my resume and phone in the other, it was a struggle to open the door. The doors were heavier than I expected, and as I was pulling, my phone began to ring. I quickly released the door handle and took a step backward from the entrance so I could see who was calling me.

As I did, I stepped into something behind me. I nearly tripped over and started falling backward, and immediately realized it wasn't a something but a someone as they graciously caught me midair.

Though at great cost to themselves because in my near tumble, my coffee slipped out of my hand and dropped behind me, and my resume fluttered to the pavement. As soon as I got my footing again, I turned around to find a stunningly handsome man standing there, his hands slowly falling from their grasp around my body. He was dressed in a phenomenal navy suit that was now covered in my spilled coffee.

To say I was mortified would be the understatement of the year.

"Oh no. Oh my gosh," I muttered to myself. "I'm so, so sorry!" In my horror, the spilled coffee paced a trail in the direction of my scattered resume, so I rushed to scoop it up from the ground, shaking the dust before stuffing it in my purse. I looked up, surprised to find this charming man still standing before me.

He was surprisingly gracious about the mishap. He looked down at his white button-down shirt, now clearly ruined with the coffee and smiled at me as he ran a hand through his perfectly-styled brown hair.

"It's no problem at all, accidents happen."

His smile only made me feel worse. I wasn't sure I'd ever seen a man this handsome in my life, not in person anyway. He looked like a damn model. Not that I'd be happy to spill coffee on anyone, but why did it have to be on a man who looked like that? Just his smile had me melting.

"Here, let me get the door for you," he said as he pulled on the ornate gold door handle. He made it look a lot more effortless than I had in my clumsiness.

"Th-thank you," I stuttered out. "I'm so sorry about the coffee. Is there anything I can do? Pay for your shirt maybe?"

I offered because it seemed like the only reasonable thing to do, but I was secretly hoping he'd say no. As I looked at his suit more closely, it was obvious to me that it was designer. I probably couldn't even afford it. So I was relieved when he shook his head.

"Nothing a good dry cleaning won't fix."

I wasn't sure about that. Coffee stains were particularly difficult to clean. But I appreciated him being so blasé about the whole thing.

"Well, again, I'm truly sorry," I said as I stepped through the door to the lobby.

"It's no problem at all. Have a wonderful day, Miss."

I smiled. "You too."

Despite living in London for several years now, I'd never quite gotten over how cute the accent was. His stunning looks were only enhanced by the sound of his voice.

As he walked away, I caught myself staring at him; though I quickly reminded myself I needed to focus. I had no time to get stuck on handsome, British men. I had to figure out which room my interview was being held in.

Even if I wasn't rushing off to a job interview, I would've never pursued a man like that anyhow. He was out of my league, and there wasn't really room in my life right now for dating. I had to focus on more important things like getting financially secure and prioritizing family. I hadn't so much as opened a dating app since my father fell ill, and I had no intention to start anytime soon.

On the wall of the lobby was a map of the hotel including all the conference rooms located on the first level My interview was down the hall and to the right in room 106.

I made my way there and was surprised to find there was a long line of chairs sitting outside room 106, and there was a person in each and every one of them.

It wasn't what I was expecting at all. I thought this would be a pretty low-key thing. I mean, it was for a tutoring job. I figured it would be me and a few other candidates at most. They really needed to interview this many people to determine who was a good fit to tutor elementary school-aged children?

These people were even richer than I thought.

I was definitely not feeling great about my chances anymore. I mean, surely one of these numerous men and women were far more qualified for the job than I was. What was supposed to make me stand out?

For a moment I almost considered walking out, but I was already here. I might as well give it a shot. I didn't want to ruin my reputation by seeming flaky, and there was the off chance that I was the tutor they were looking for.

I sat next to a petite blonde woman with shoulder-length hair. She had her legs purposefully crossed. I smiled as I considered asking her if she knew why there were so many applicants.

She didn't meet my smile and instead kept a serious expression and looked forward. Okay, so it didn't look like I'd be making any friends today. I sat patiently as candidates were called back only to return quickly thereafter with their shoulders slumped and disappointment written all over their faces. This only intensified my anxiety, but I resolved to give the best interview I could, the need of resolving my financial issues was too great for me to just walk away without a fight.

A small, stout, middle-aged woman exited the room and looked down at a clipboard in front of her.

"Is there a Maggie here?" she asked.

Oh, crap! Me already? There was still a large line in front of me, and it didn't seem as though I'd been waiting very long. The air of doom circulated the hallway, but I gave fear an internal pep talk before standing tall and proud, shoulders back, straightened my skirt and greeted the woman with a friendly smile. Like the woman I had sat next to outside, she didn't meet that smile and instead retained a serious demeanor. I tried not to allow that to make me nervous, but it definitely did. I followed at a cautious distance to prevent any further mishaps such as that of my arrival.

She took a seat behind the long walnut table and motioned toward the chair across from her. I sat with my back ram-rod straight, ankles crossed and looked up at the woman and man who stared back at me. I let out an involuntary gasp before sucking the sudden anxiety in. well huh. A smirk splayed wide across his face as his brow rose into his hairline, a hint of curiosity in his gaze.

It was the man I'd spilled my coffee on! Crap, crap, crap! What was he doing here?

Well, if I wasn't already positive I wasn't getting the job, I was convinced now.

The woman looked at me with a furrowed brow. "Is there something wrong?" she asked in response to my gasp, her tone pointed.

"N-no." I looked at the man blankly, wondering if he would rat me out.

I realized immediately, of course, that they

15

probably weren't husband and wife. He seemed too young for the woman. He was certainly closer to my age than hers.

He didn't rat me out but instead extended his hand. "You must be Maggie."

"Yes, hello." I shook his hand in response and then reached out to shake the woman's.

"Hello, Maggie. I am Ms. Mitchell. It's very good to meet you."

The name seemed familiar, but I couldn't place the woman outside of a vague feeling of familiarity.

Who were they? Perhaps assistants of the family who wanted to hire a tutor. How important could these people be that they wouldn't attend the interview themselves, though? Not that I'd ever say that because I wanted this job, but I was most definitely judging them already.

"Do you have your resume, dear?" Ms. Mitchell asked.

"Oh, yes, of course!" I said as I pulled it out of my purse.

Embarrassingly, it had become a bit crinkled in

there, a slight smattering of dust staining the back of the page. I tried to flatten it on the table as I did my best to keep myself from blushing.

This was an epic failure. My ears were getting hot from the stress, my blood pressure skyrocketing. I was really flubbing this whole thing.

"Ah, so you studied early childhood development in college?" she asked.

"I did, yes. I love children." I smiled warmly, though I was inadvertently avoiding eye contact with the man.

I shouldn't have been. I mean, it was just as much an interview with him as it was with her. I couldn't contain my embarrassment.

"When will you be receiving your degree?" the man, who had still yet to identify himself, asked me.

Dammit, I was hoping they wouldn't ask that.

"Well, uh, actually ... I won't be. I had to drop out of school due to some unfortunate personal circumstances."

"You are American, are you?" Ms. Mitchell asked.

"Yes, born and raised. However, I've been in London for a couple of years," I told her.

"Do you know much about the royal family?" she asked.

"A bit," I tried to lie.

The lie was pretty blatant. I'd never been one to pay attention to celebrities. To me, European royalty were essentially just celebrities. I wasn't sure why I should retain an interest in the lives of total strangers.

"So you are familiar with the royal children? Abigail and Andrew?"

"Ah, yes. Abigail and Andrew, of course." I forced a smile.

She looked at me skeptically. "What grade is Abigail in now?" she asked.

"Uh … third?" I guessed.

The disappointment on her face was obvious. "She's in fifth."

"Ah … yeah. Uh, well… Admittedly, I don't know much about the children. It's more the queen I've read about. I mean, it's kind of creepy to put children in the spotlight in my opinion. So I don't really go out of my way to read about them."

There was an immediate awkward tension in the air, and I couldn't tell why. Was it something I'd said?

"My dear, you do know this is a position to tutor the children of the royal family, don't you?"

My jaw dropped. "No... Uh, no. I wasn't aware of that."

Well, I looked like an absolute idiot now. If I'd known, I would've brushed up on information about the royal family. The only thing royal I knew at the moment was that I'd royally screwed this up.

"I'm sorry. I'm truly sorry. I'm just a very busy person and don't have the time to keep up on current events. It's hard enough for me to follow American politics."

Ms. Mitchell nodded. "It's quite alright, I just wanted to make sure you knew. Let's continue, shall we?"

"Mmhmm," I said through clenched lips. I had no idea how I was going to survive the rest of this interview when I'd already made such a fool of myself.

Ms. Mitchell cleared her throat. "Have you worked with children in the past?"

"Oh, yes, definitely. I was a nanny for a while. I was actually an au pair briefly—that was how I was able to move to London to study abroad in the first place."

"How do you like London?" she asked.

"Oh, I absolutely love it. London is great."

"How long have you lived here again?" the man asked.

"Several years. Since college."

"And for what reason did you decide to stay in London? Do you simply prefer London? Or perhaps you met someone?"

I felt my cheeks warm with a blush. Did he just ask me if I had a boyfriend? Well I'd set him straight.

"I fell in love." I smiled lovingly. "With the glorious charm of London. The architecture, landscape, culture—that is why I stayed. My only love affair is with the city."

"So you haven't met anyone then?" he challenged with a smirk. Had I not just answered that question?

Ms. Mitchell stared at him with as much confusion as I was experiencing. "I don't think that's an appropriate question."

"Right, of course." He nodded, to my relief. "Next question then… Do you have any children of your own?"

"Edward!" Ms. Mitchell reprimanded him.

Well, at least now I knew his name.

"What?" Edward asked with a mischievous smile. "That seemed like a pertinent question to me. We're trying to assess how she is with children, correct?"

"We don't need to know about her family situation to assess that," Ms. Mitchell said sternly.

"No, that's quite alright," I spoke up. "I don't have children, though I hope to one day. I just haven't met the right person."

He smiled at me. "Interesting."

Ms. Mitchell looked at him sternly, and he

looked back with a jerk of his head. They were communicating but not verbally.

From that point forward, Edward remained silent as Ms. Mitchell continued the interview. The final questions were a lot less personal in nature.

I didn't feel that any of my answers were redeeming. At the end of the interview, I thanked them both for their time, I knew I wasn't going to get the job.

I left disappointed but not altogether surprised. Especially not after discovering that it was the royal children they were looking for someone to tutor. It made complete sense to me now why there were so many applicants. There were certainly many more qualified people in that room than me, particularly when it came to knowledge on the royal family. Frankly, I wasn't sure why they'd even entertain interviewing an American.

When I got home, the first thing I did was go to my father's bedroom to check on him. I didn't like to leave him alone for more than an hour at a time these days. I had a caregiver some days who came to help with him, but nobody was coming in today.

To my relief, he was asleep. Good, he needed to be resting. I shut the door quietly and exited the room.

I wasn't exactly looking forward to telling him I didn't get the job. He had been so hopeful when I left. Despite his illness, he was always incredibly positive about everything. That was something I couldn't relate to. As the days went by and he became more ill, I only felt more and more negative.

Though I did my best not to appear positive and upbeat.

I went to the kitchen to see what I could make for dinner. I had some thawed chicken breasts in the fridge that I forgot I had put out the night before and decided to season those and put them in the oven to bake.

As the chicken cooked, I looked at the mail on the kitchen table. The caregiver must have brought it up the night before without my noticing. I flipped through it. It was mostly junk, but then I realized we'd received another letter from the hospital.

No, not a letter … a bill.

I sighed as I looked at the costs. I really had hoped I'd get this job so that these bills would stop piling up. It was so damn overwhelming.

It looked as if I was going to be overwhelmed for the foreseeable future.

Chapter 2

Edward

"You are such a giant asshole!"

I heard the high heel shoe coming toward me before I saw it. Even though it was coming from behind me, I ducked. I was expecting it.

"An absolute dog! Do you not have any self-respect?"

I turned around and smiled. "Some, yeah."

"Get the hell out of here!" she snapped at me.

"Cecilia, I don't know why you're overreacting. I never said that we were together."

"You never said it? Six months of my life, Edward. Six months! Of course I thought we were exclusive."

"Well, you thought wrong. We were just dating. It's not like I ever said I loved you or anything."

"It was implied!" she yelled out again.

"By who?" I asked on a chuckle.

"Ugh!" She threw her other shoe at me. "Get out of here before I call your mum and tell her what a cad you are!"

"Gladly," I muttered. I didn't want her to dig any further into her shoe collection.

Besides, I had somewhere to be. I was already running late for a series of interviews I had to assist Ms. Mitchell with. I shouldn't have spent so much time at Cecilia's this morning, but I didn't expect that I was going to have to explain to her that we weren't actually together.

She was livid, but honestly, I didn't think I'd done anything wrong. We weren't an official anything. A fling. We had casual fun, as I had with all the ladies I courted, and were nothing more. Frankly, I never would have made things official with her. Not that I had the intention of making things official with anyone.

I liked to date around. It suited my lifestyle more. Whenever felt things were getting a little too serious with a woman, I took the time to bow out.

I hoped Ms. Mitchell wouldn't be too mad

about the fact that I was late. She was head of domestic work for my family, and I knew she wouldn't hesitate to tattle to my mother regarding my *bad* behavior.

Not that I cared too much about that, but I had enough trouble from my mother as it was. She was constantly urging me to be more responsible. She insisted I needed to stop partying and take my responsibilities to the crown more seriously. I would eventually inherit the throne after all.

Hard to imagine, me as King. I couldn't commit to a relationship, never mind being head of the royal family. But I was the oldest. I always knew that day would come.

That was probably the reason why I was so steadfast about partying and shirking my responsibilities. One day, my life would be consumed of only my responsibilities to the crown and the people of my country. There would be no way I could decide to screw off and fly to the Bahamas with some friends for a few weeks. I wouldn't have the freedom to do as I wished. I needed to get all that out of my system now.

I'd tried to explain that to my mother many times over, but she didn't seem concerned. She reminded me that the country needed to see me as someone trustworthy, amenable. She believed I was ruining my reputation.

Who cared about my reputation? I was inheriting the throne regardless. It wasn't as if they needed to vote me in. Who cared if the people liked me?

I had my driver drop me off outside of the hotel where we were conducting interviews. I was looking down at my watch and trying to evaluate how late I was when I felt hot liquid pour down my suit.

It took a second to process, and, admittedly, I was pretty damn angry at whoever spilled something on me. I looked up quickly and found a small form stumbling backward. I reacted in an instant and latched out to stabilize her. She found her footing and twisted toward me, her mouth agape in a shock of horror. I assessed the blue-eyed beauty standing in front of me and calmed down considerably.

She was gorgeous, and I couldn't deny I had a

weak spot for gorgeous women.

"Oh no. Oh my gosh," she muttered to herself. "I'm so, so sorry!"

Her voice was just about as cute as she was. She wasn't British, that much was clear. She had a very pronounced American accent. The only thing that made me more forgiving than gorgeous women were gorgeous American women.

I expected that once she took in my face, she'd realize who I was, and her apologies would become even greater. Not every day that you spilled coffee all over a prince after all.

Even as she stared into my eyes, she didn't seem to notice who I was.

"It's no problem at all, accidents happen," I told her with a smile.

She was quiet for a moment, and I thought maybe she was beginning to process who I was. Which was a bit of a bummer for me since it wasn't often I got to interact with people who didn't realize they were speaking to British royalty.

"Here, let me get the door for you," I told her

before she had a chance make introductions.

"Thank you. I'm so sorry about the coffee. Is there anything I can do? Pay for your shirt, maybe?" she asked.

Pay for my shirt? Huh. Maybe she hadn't realized who I was. I could certainly purchase another bloody shirt.

"Nothing a good dry cleaning won't fix," I reassured her.

"Well, again, I'm truly sorry," she said as she stepped in front of me as I held the door.

"It's no problem at all. Have a wonderful day, Miss."

The last thing I wanted to do was say my good-byes. This woman had intrigued me. I wished I could speak to her longer, but I was already running too late.

She smiled. "You too."

I rushed past her into the conference room where Ms. Mitchell was waiting for me. She looked at me disapprovingly.

"You almost didn't make it, Prince Edward,"

she told me.

"Just a hectic morning, Ms. Mitchell. But despite what you'd like to believe, I do attempt to uphold the few responsibilities Mother has assigned to me."

She didn't seem convinced that was true, but she didn't argue it. Then she noticed the dark liquid that had permeated my shirt.

"Edward, really? You couldn't at least show up in a clean shirt?" she asked.

"This happened right outside. Some young, distracted woman spilled her coffee all over me. It was unavoidable."

"Very well. You know there will be some people that leave this interview, and the first thing they'll do is report back to some atrocious gossip magazine, who will have an entire article tomorrow about how disheveled you looked, speculating on the events of the night prior."

"So, let them speculate," I said. "It's nothing more than that."

"Unless, of course, you truly were getting into

some debauchery the night prior," she accused.

"I wasn't," I assured her.

Even though I completely was.

"Are you ready to call in the first interviewee?" she asked.

"Fire away." I smiled as I took my seat.

The first few interviews were cut and dry. Candidates with all the qualifications of which Mother desired—well-educated, punctual, uptight, and boorish. I'd have fallen asleep by now if Ms. Mitchell hadn't been kicking me under the table to keep me awake. As the last candidate left the room, the concierge brought in mugs of tea while Ms. Mitchell left the table.

I pulled my phone out of my pocket and turned around slightly to look at it, wondering if I had any messages from Cecilia. I didn't want Ms. Mitchell coming back and being able to see my phone, so I shifted a bit to hide.

There were no messages, to my relief. Hopefully we could move forward from this situation amicably.

I heard the chair scrape against the floor and felt movement beside me, so I put my phone in my pocket and turned my attention toward the next interview. I started ahead for a moment, stunned. Before me with her legs crossed at the ankles, looking like a deer caught in the headlights, was the woman who spilled coffee on me this morning.

I had been dreading these interviews, but, hey, if this gave me the opportunity to talk to her, I could handle it.

Ms. Mitchell started off right away by asking her about the royal family. Which should have been interesting because based on the fact that she still hadn't seemed to recognize me, I would guess she knew very little about the royal family.

She lied, tried to pretend that she did. Ms. Mitchell tried to quiz her on what grade my little sister Abigail was in. She failed miserably.

It had become pretty clear, not just to me but to Ms. Mitchell as well, that not only did this Maggie girl know nothing about the royal family, but she wasn't even aware that she was going to potentially be hired by the royal family.

"My dear, you do know this is a position to tutor the children of the royal family, don't you?"

Her jaw dropped. "No... Uh, no. I wasn't aware of that."

She was flustered, but it only served to make her look even cuter. I wasn't sure what it was about this woman, I found her absolutely adorable.

"I'm sorry. I'm truly sorry. I'm just a very busy person and don't have the time to keep up on current events. It's hard enough for me to follow American politics."

Ms. Mitchell nodded. "It's quite alright, I just wanted to make sure you knew. Let's continue, shall we?"

Ms. Mitchell proceeded to ask a few dull questions about her qualifications, something I couldn't have cared less about. Not that I'd say it aloud, but this entire interview process seemed so stupid to me. We didn't need to hold such extensive interviews for just a tutor. My brother and sister may have been royalty, but that didn't mean they needed this much attention over their damn education—not at their ages. Education was important, but they were still children. Royal children at that.

I had other questions I was interested in asking her, though they had nothing to do with her qualifications.

" Why did you decide to stay in London?" She's already explained she'd came to London for school, but I was interested in what—or rather who if there was someone—had kept her here, so far away from home. "Do you simply prefer London? Or perhaps you met someone?"

I saw no reason not to burst out and ask. I was curious… Was she single? This seemed like as good a time as any to find out.

Her face grew red from the question, once again endearing her to me.

"I don't think that's an appropriate question," Ms. Mitchell scolded me, making her disapproval quite obvious.

"Right, of course." I nodded, though I had no

intention of stopping my line of questioning. "Next question, then… Do you have any children of your own?"

"Edward!" Ms. Mitchell yelled at me.

I grinned at her.

"What? That seemed like a pertinent question to me. We're trying to assess how she is with children, correct?"

"We don't need to know about her family situation to assess that," Ms. Mitchell told me.

"Um, no, that's alright." She surprised me by speaking up. "I don't have children, though I hope to one day. I just haven't met the right person."

"Interesting," I answered, being quite obvious about my interest in her.

Ms. Mitchell had had enough of me. She kicked me under the table again, this time right in the shin. I couldn't deny it hurt. For an older woman, she had a powerful leg.

I looked over at her, and she continued to stare me down, willing me to behave.

It worked. As much as I'd have liked to ignore

her, I couldn't deny she had some authority over me. I would behave in the interview from there on out.

I allowed Ms. Mitchell to do the rest of the talking. I had no questions about Maggie's qualifications anyway. I did, however, hope Ms. Mitchell would continue to question her at length. As professional as always, she questioned Maggie only on her education and experiences in education and working with children. The luster of the moment faded even further from my grasp when the interview ended, I found myself quite disappointed. I didn't want Maggie to leave. There was still so much about this lovely woman that had yet to learn.

"Well, thank you so much for seeing me. I appreciate you two taking the time on behalf of the royal family." She extended a hand to Ms. Mitchell and then to me.

It was another mistake on her part, of course. I wasn't here on behalf of the royal family—I was the royal family. She'd likely be embarrassed all over again to discover that she had been talking to the Prince of England this entire time. Even more so that she had spilled coffee on me.

For a moment, I considered telling her that fact because of how cute she looked every time she was caught off guard. Ultimately I decided against it. I was kind of hoping she would get the job, and I didn't want to mess with her chances.

"She's the one," I told Ms. Mitchell as soon as Maggie had left.

"The one for what? For you to pursue? I think all women are 'the one' in that regard, Edward," she said, frustrated. "Behave yourself from now on. I don't want to see you acting up around any other attractive young women."

"No, I obviously mean the one for the job," I told her.

Ms. Mitchell eyed me. "She handled your ridiculousness quite well; I'll give her that. Perhaps it is an indication that she'd be able to handle the children."

Good, so she was at least in the running. I would have very much liked to see her again, not that I was going to tell Ms. Mitchell that. It would have been a guarantee for her not to get hired.

"I mean, do we really need to sit through the rest of the interviews at this point?" I asked.

"Of course, we do. We made these appointments, and we will finish them. It would be entirely rude to dismiss the rest of the applicants. Besides, there may very well be someone more qualified for the job here."

That was what I was afraid of. I didn't want to find someone more qualified for the job. I wanted Maggie to get the job.

"You know, she may not have known much about the royal family, but you can consider that a benefit, don't you think?"

She seemed to consider this briefly before asking, "How so?"

"Well, a lot of these people have applied strictly because it's a job with the royal family. Like you said earlier, they won't hesitate to report to tabloids. You can be sure that Maggie never came into this interview with any intention to gossip about the family. She clearly has no ulterior motives."

"Hmm, yes, I do suppose that's true," Ms. Mitchell acknowledged.

I could see it on her face—I'd made a good point and had got Maggie one step closer to the job.

Chapter 3

Maggie

I looked up at the absolutely massive castle in front of me as I tried to process that this was where I'd now be working.

Nobody had been more surprised than me to hear that I'd gotten the job.

I was nearly in a state of shock when I'd answered the call. I was sitting down to dinner with my father, and I actually squealed in excitement when I hung up. I felt bad because I was sure I had startled him badly, but after I told him the reason for my excitement, he was jumping for joy with me.

Not literally, of course. Poor man couldn't jump if his life depended on it right now. Internally, we were both jumping. That medical bill I'd received a few days prior felt less daunting with this new position.

The caregiver would now be with my father

during all my work hours. It was a few hours more than she was used to coming, but I could supplement that now. All I had to do was manage to keep this job, and I'd have less stress to deal with.

Though, that might be easier said than done. It was still beyond me how I'd even gotten the job in the first place. I most definitely couldn't have been the most qualified person to apply. And the way I had truly messed up answering about the details of the royal family... That was a disaster.

I'd done my research since then, of course. Abigail was ten-years-old, and Andrew was twelve. They apparently had an older brother, Edward, but I didn't think it was relevant because I most definitely wouldn't be tutoring him. He was in his twenties. I wondered a bit about the large age gap, but it wasn't as if I'd ever get the chance to ask anyone about it.

The doorman waiting outside let me in with a smile.

"You must be Maggie," he said. "May I see some ID?"

This threw me off at first, but of course they

would need to see my ID. Couldn't let any old person just waltz into the castle, could you?

Or, wait … was it called a castle? A palace? I was really out of my element with this whole royal thing. Apparently, I didn't do as much research as I initially thought.

I walked inside and was greeted by Ms. Mitchell.

"Maggie, hello. Come along and follow me." She was polite but always maintained her somewhat stern demeanor. I immediately felt like she was an authority figure. I could say that for sure.

"You are always going to be working with the children in this room. You are to be here and prepared to begin instructions before they finish with their classes for the day, which is at one pm. They have a very tight schedule but will have two hours with you each day. You will go over all the work they did with their teachers and then subsequently take them to their horseback riding lessons at the stables. During those lessons is when you will take your break. You will eat your dinner with the rest of the staff in the dining quarters. After that, you will meet directly with their teachers to discuss their work."

"Wait, I meet with their teachers … every day? Here?" I asked. "Aren't they, like, busy with other students?"

Ms. Mitchell laughed. "Well, no, of course not. They only work with Prince Andrew and Princess Abigail. They have no other students."

I couldn't help but think how lonely this sounded.

Many of my best memories were at public school growing up. Although, admittedly, there were plenty of awful memories too, particularly in middle school; but it was where I made all my friends. It was where I was happy to go when I was sick of my parents and sick of being at home.

What did Andrew and Abigail get to do when they wanted out of the house? They didn't have even a semblance of a normal life.

I didn't envy them that was for sure.

We walked up a long spiral staircase. It was gorgeous with beautiful red ornate carpet running

44

down it. Though once we reached a certain height, it made me very queasy to look down at the tile of the foyer below. I'd never been a fan of heights.

We reached a room that had a square wooden table in the middle of it with one chair on one side and two chairs on the other. The walls were lined with bookshelves; I wasn't even sure how many books were in this room. Surely it had to have been thousands. Would we really be accessing these books during our tutoring sessions? I didn't ask.

"The prince and princess will be in shortly." Ms., Mitchell smiled.

"I can't wait to meet them," I said.

Everything about this job had me nervous. I felt horribly out of place here, and I felt like everyone could tell I was a fraud. I was particularly afraid that the children were going to sense it. They'd see right through me. Maybe they'd even report back to their mother and tell her I wasn't the right one to work with them.

I tried to hide my nervousness as we waited for the prince and princess to walk in. I didn't want to look like I was entirely out of my element, though I definitely was. It was a weird feeling, to be afraid of kids so young, but I felt like they were superior to me. They were royalty!

When the prince and princess walked in, Ms. Mitchell spoke again.

"This is Prince Andrew, though he prefers Drew, and Princess Abigail. Children, this is Miss Maggie. She is to be your new tutor."

Miss Maggie … it sounded so formal.

I gave a little bow. "Lovely to meet you, Your Royal Highnesses."

I already sounded incredibly stupid.

They both chuckled a bit. Good… Glad I'd made a proper fool of myself already.

"She's funny." Abigail chuckled.

She was a cute little girl. She had curly brown hair that fell in large ringlets around her shoulders. It was like if Shirley Temple was brunette, not something you commonly saw these days.

"Glad I can entertain." I smiled, as if I'd made a fool of myself on purpose. I most certainly didn't.

"Yes, she is quite funny," Ms. Mitchell agreed.

"You're an American?" Drew asked, a little incredulous. "Will an American be able to properly teach us about European history?"

He had the same hair color as his sister, and it was properly styled in a part on the right side of his head.

"I'm very happy to hear you're so interested in European history," I told them, "because I studied it for many years when I was going to university. I happened to go to university here in London, so I like to think I learned from the best."

He smiled a bit, contented with that answer. I looked over to see Ms. Mitchell's reaction and sensed she approved of our rapport so far.

"Alright, then. Now that we've had our introductions, let's get straight to work. Maggie, I will be in with you to help tutor today. I have been tutoring the children for the past month after their last tutor quit."

"Yeah, he couldn't keep up," Drew said, a little bitingly.

47

"Prince Drew," Ms. Mitchell reprimanded, "we should not speak ill of those who are not here to defend themselves."

"Not that he could defend himself..." Drew rolled his eyes, and Abigail chuckled.

Well, the pressure was now certainly on me to perform. It was clear that Drew was wise beyond his years, and he wasn't going to be satisfied if it wasn't obvious that I knew what I was talking about.

I'd been very studious in school, and I was a bookworm when I was his age. Hopefully I'd be up to the task.

I mostly watched as Ms. Mitchell went over everything the kids had been learning. Abigail found herself drifting off pretty often, but Drew was zoned in on her every word. I was sure I'd even caught Abigail doodling a few times, though I didn't admonish her for it.

Two hours later, it was time for their riding lessons. Ms. Mitchell led me and the children out to the stables. It wouldn't be hard to remember how to get to them—there was a long trail from the castle to the stables made out of paved stones.

I wished that I could catch a glimpse of the kids riding since I'd never ridden a horse myself, but Ms. Mitchell promptly took me back to the castle to show me where the dining quarters were. I resolved that when it was just me and the kids, I'd linger a little before I went to take my break.

There was only one person in the dining quarters when we entered. She was around my age, maybe a little older, with long blonde hair tied into a braid that fell down her back. She was in a traditional maid's uniform—all black with a white collar and white buttons.

"Millie, this is Maggie," Ms. Mitchell announced as we entered. "She is the new tutor. I was just showing her where the staff eats on their lunch and dinner breaks."

She extended her hand to me. "Maggie, hello. So nice to see a new face around here." She smiled warmly.

Something about her put me at ease. Everything and every person in this castle so far had felt so prim and proper. Millie was the first person who felt like she could be just another woman I ran into on the street.

Ms. Mitchell left me to eat, and I pulled out some of the snacks I'd had in my purse.

"You know, they have loads of food in the kitchen that we're allowed access to, if you'd rather have that," Millie told me as she watched me open the trail mix.

"Oh, no, I'm fine with this, but thank you," I told her.

"So how did you end up with the tutoring job?" she asked as she took a bite of her salad. "I was surprised to hear the American accent."

"Oh, well, to be honest, I'm not sure." I laughed. "I really feel like I lucked into the position. When I left the interview, I thought for sure I had ruined the entire thing. Nobody was more surprised than me that they'd actually decided to hire me. Not that I'm not relieved, of course. I'm truly appreciative. I really needed this job."

"It does pay well, doesn't it?" she asked. "I

never dreamt myself a maid as a little girl, but when I saw what they were willing to pay here, I applied straightaway. I can't get paid better anywhere else without an education."

"Yeah, I'm pretty much in the same boat," I told her. "I had to quit school early when my dad got sick, so I never actually got my degree. I flew him out here because even with our medical insurance back home, it seemed like medical care would be cheaper here. Not that we get it for free like you guys, of course, but it's still more affordable. I'm hoping this job will be enough to help cover those costs."

I hadn't realized how much I'd said until it was too late. I wasn't sure why it was so easy to open up to Millie. She had a warmth about her. She felt like an old friend.

"I'm so sorry to hear about your dad. Will he be alright?"

"I hope so. He has cancer, unfortunately." I smiled, trying to play off the situation. "He's in good spirits, and he's responding to treatment."

"So glad to hear that. You're so young to have

to be taking care of your father that way. I can't imagine how hard that would be."

"It's hard. He does make it easier by being such a ray of shining positivity. I've got to hand it to him for that. Don't know how I'd stay so positive if I was in his position."

As I continued to talk to Millie and eat my snacks, I started to feel less out of place here. I had a feeling I was going to actually enjoy this job, especially if I was able to make new friends along the way.

Chapter 4

Edward

I strolled through the hallways of the palace mindlessly, bored and tired of waiting for the hours to tick by.

It was Maggie's first day, and if I was being honest, I was just waiting for a moment to barge in on her.

She hadn't left my mind since the interview. Which was strange because girls didn't usually stay stuck in my brain all that long.

I felt like perhaps this was something I had to get out of my system. Like I'd seen her, I'd liked her, and now I'd need to pursue her to get her out of my head. That was how it often went for me. What could I say? I was a man who always loved the chase.

I knew I couldn't barge in on my brother and sister's tutoring lesson, of course. Ms. Mitchell would never allow it and would cast me out immediately. Although, even if she didn't, I wouldn't exactly want Abigail and Drew to see me flirting with their tutor.

Abigail and Drew were the only members of this family who still thought highly of me. All the adults knew better. They saw me as an irresponsible young man with no vision for his life. They were right about that.

Abigail and Drew still worshipped me, like little siblings often did. They saw me as their invincible big brother. I could do no wrong to them. I did my best to seem like I had it all together around them. They'd never seen me drunk or flirtatious. In their eyes, I actually was a responsible young adult. My mom didn't have the heart to tell them otherwise.

At this point in the day, though, Abigail and Drew were most certainly with their riding instructor. Where would that leave Maggie at this exact moment?

I walked out to the stables and didn't see her anywhere, though Abigail caught a glimpse of me and waved eagerly from her horse. I waved back and was pretty impressed with how good she had become. She was a natural.

Especially compared to Drew, who had always been a bit clumsy and likely always would be. It took him a long time to adjust to horseback riding, and I knew he still hated it.

Well, if Maggie wasn't out at the stables with the kids that had to mean she was on her break. I went to the dining quarters, though I normally spent no time there.

Sure enough, she was there with one of our maids, Millie. It looked like another maid, Annabelle, was just pulling up a chair to sit when I got there.

I waltzed over confidently to them.

"Hello, ladies." I smiled at Annabelle and Millie first because they were facing me. Maggie had her back turned to me, so I walked around the table and took a seat next to Millie so I was facing her.

Annabelle and Millie both straightened their spines, noticeably uncomfortable in my presence. I expected this. I was used to the staff's demeanor becoming tense around me. Not that I was mean or rude to any of them or anything. I wasn't at all strict or demanding. I personally couldn't have cared less if they did or didn't do their jobs.

Still, in their eyes, I'd always be one of the bosses. Nobody wanted to eat dinner with the boss.

"Oh, hello. Nice to see you again." Maggie smiled casually. She hadn't yet noticed the other's discomfort.

Did this mean that she still hadn't figured out who I was? Even after learning she was going to be working for the royals, did she not even do a cursory Google search?

No matter, though. Her obliviousness would only make flirting with her more fun.

"Yes, still here. I often am." I smiled.

"What is it that you do for the royal family?" she asked, as she fished her hand into a bag of trail mix and pulled out a raisin.

Both Annabelle and Millie became even more

uncomfortable at hearing this. Millie was first to excuse herself.

"Uh, I think I'm … done for now." She grabbed her plate and stood.

"Yeah, me too." Annabelle stood as well.

"Annabelle, you just sat down!" I teased.

She ignored this as she and Millie scurried away, leaving Maggie confused.

"Do they not like you or something?" she asked.

"Oh, I would assume they like me quite fine," I told her, not extrapolating further. Her confusion was cute, and I was going to savor it.

"How are you liking the new job?" I asked.

"It's very nice. Certainly, pays very well, though I'm sure you knew that." She looked at me curiously. "How did someone as young as you manage to get a position with the royal family were you're responsible for hiring on new people?"

"Oh, don't worry yourself about that," I brushed it off. "So, where in America are you from?"

"The west coast," she answered, not giving

57

more of an answer than that.

"What year did you move to London?"

She paused before answering. "Oh, am I still being interviewed for the position?" she asked. "I thought I'd already went through that process and done splendidly."

I was impressed by her quick wit. I loved a clever woman. Though, of course, I would have to respond with some snark of my own.

"Splendidly? Were we at the same interview?" I teased.

"Well, I did get the job," she pointed out proudly.

"Thanks to yours truly. You're welcome, by the way."

She eyed me. "You wanted to hire me?"

"I did. I made a very compelling case to Ms. Mitchell about it. In fact, I told her that your absolute and total failure of knowing details about the royal family was actually a positive attribute."

"How so?" She furrowed her brow.

"Well, if you didn't know anything about the

royal family, that had to mean you weren't here to spy on them, right? That you had no ill intentions? You were just a woman looking for a well-paying tutoring job. Every other interviewee we saw that day was extremely well-versed on the details of the royal family. So how could we be sure their intentions were pure?"

I could see clarity befall her face. This made sense to her. She'd probably been wondering for a while now how she was able to get the job with absolutely no royal knowledge. Well, now she knew it was thanks to me.

"Why did you fight so hard to get me hired?" she asked, a little incredulous.

"I found you interesting. I was hoping I'd see you around. Perhaps ask some questions and get to learn you better."

"Learn me, huh?" She rolled her eyes. "Well, I'm not too keen on being learned."

I leaned over the table, giving her a winning smile. "You're a tutor. Helping people learn is what you do. Can't you help me?"

"I'm only here to help the royal children learn." She put her foot down.

She definitely wasn't caving to me just because she learned I'd helped her get the job. That was fine, I wouldn't have expected her to. I was once again impressed by her attitude.

Though talking to her wasn't exactly quelling my desires. The more she shut me down, the more I wanted to pursue her.

My phone buzzed in my pocket, and I pulled it out, annoyed. I didn't want to be distracted further from Maggie, but I answered anyway.

"Hello?"

"Are we still on for tonight?" I heard Angelique's voice ask me.

Shit, I had completely forgotten.

I'd been seeing Angelique for a month or so now. She was pretty and I liked her, though it wasn't anything serious.

I looked down at my watch. I was supposed to meet her in an hour. Which meant I should have been getting ready to leave now.

"Oh, uh…" I muttered.

"Seriously, Edward? We had plans. You were finally going to take me out to dinner."

This was something she'd been wanting for a while. I'd kept things pretty low-key with her, never going out on any actual dates since I had been seeing Cecilia as well, but she insisted she only wanted to go out to eat sometime. She said that she knew it didn't mean anything more, so I'd agreed.

But … right now? I didn't want to leave Maggie.

"Let me call you right back, okay?" I answered noncommittally.

"Edward, you'd better not—"

I had already hung up and turned my attention back to Maggie.

"So, you're off in a few hours, right?" I knew the routine of the tutors because I'd also had one. Next she had to talk to the kids' teachers.

"I am," she said, as she looked down at her trail mix and paid little attention to me.

"Any chance you'd be interested in me taking

61

you out after?" I grinned at her.

She may have been pushing away my advances so far, but I had assumed she was playing hard to get. I felt like we had some chemistry and that she was interested.

So I was surprised when she simply said no.

"No? Just ... no? No explanation?"

"Just no," she repeated on a shrug.

Well, that stung.

I was quiet for a moment, trying to figure out my next move. I had no intention of giving up—not now. No way. Her rejection only made me want her more. I couldn't even remember the last time I'd been rejected. When you were the prince, it didn't happen often.

So, I had to think… What could potentially get me closer to Maggie?

I nodded and turned my back on Maggie as I pulled out my phone and called Angelique back.

"Hello?" she answered roughly.

"Hey. Sorry about that, I was caught up in a conversation with a new member of the staff. Of course we're on for tonight. I'll see you in an hour."

"Oh, okay." Her tone immediately changed. "I'll see you then."

"Great, see you."

I hung up and turned to look at Maggie, trying to gauge her reaction. I was hoping it would make her jealous.

If it did, she really gave no inclination of that. She kept eating her trail mix, straight-faced.

"Prince Edward?" I heard a voice say from behind me. "What are you doing here?"

I turned around to see one of our butlers, Raymond, walking over to the table.

"Oh, I was strolling through the palace when I ran into our new tutor, Miss Maggie, and thought we'd have our introductions. I was actually just on my way out, though," I said as I continued to stare at Maggie.

"Well is there anything I can get you before your departure, Your Highness?"

"That won't be necessary, Raymond, but I do appreciate it. I was actually just on my way out. I have a date with Miss Bennett."

Raymond's eyes widened as he hid a mischievous grin. That was one thing the old coot did enjoy, hearing drab details about my personal life—the various women I courted. He always said he didn't understand how I carried on precariously while bequeathed the heir to the throne without my name being dragged through the mud, but the fact is—the paparazzi would sell any bloody tale that involved a royal and scandalous deeds.

Raymond continued through the palace, leaving Maggie and I in the stark silence of her newest revelation.

"Wait... Prince Edward?" she asked, her bottom lip wobbling. "As in *The* Prince Edward of England?"

My smirk grew into a smile as I replied, "That's right. I guess that means you actually can help me to learn you, right? I mean, if you're going to tutor all the queen's children..."

I laughed as I got up from the table, dismissing our conversation, though I doubted Maggie could find the words for a rebuttal—her mouth was hung wide is shock and awe.

I strolled from the room, before she had a chance to gather herself, taking just a moment to look over my shoulder and offer her a slight wink.

MCKENNA JAMES

Chapter 5

Maggie

I came into work the next day, honestly unsure if I even had a job.

Once again, I'd made a complete and total fool of myself. I knew that the older prince was named Edward. Even though I'd never seen him before my interview, why didn't I piece it together? How could I not have realized he was the prince?

I had been kind of a bitch to the Prince of England. Like, the prince who was one day going to be the King.

However, he did deserve it, though. He was being totally presumptuous. The first time I'd met him, I thought he was so sweet and charming, but I could see now, he was conceited and entitled. Imagine that—a filthy rich, playboy prince who was conceited and entitled. Yeah, I was fully within my rights to reject him.

I wouldn't have been so rude about it had I known. I would have given him the respect he deserved as prince while letting him down gently. Did he deserve anything less? I'm completely torn in that regard. Now, however, I completely understood why Millie and the other maid, who I had not yet met, were so quick to leave. Nobody wanted to eat with the boss around.

Well, if I did get fired, I'd one day be able to tell my future kids their mom got fired after rejecting the King of England. That would be one hell of a story.

I really didn't want to lose my job.,. Not just because I needed the money, but because I was really excited to work with Princess Abigail and Prince Drew. I had always loved childcare and helping children grow through education and enrichment made my job all the more enjoyable. I knew it was corny to say, but I was a strong believer that children were the future, and I loved making connections with them. It felt like I was helping to build the future world.

In this case, I truly might have been. These

children were going to be leaders one day. They were going to have more power than I ever would, and I got to help shape how they learned. That was pretty awesome.

I waited patiently for Abigail and Drew to enter the room. When they did, I sat up straight and tried to put on my best authoritative face.

"Prince Drew, Princess Abigail. Great to see you. Have a seat. I know we went over a bit of what you were learning yesterday, but I really want to assess where you guys are at. So can you tell me what subjects you're learning about in each class? Where are you each in science, for example?"

I had a notebook out in front of me and was prepared to takes notes to help gather where they were academically. I wanted to seem wholly professional when I visited with their teachers later.

Drew was the first to speak up. "I just learned about Darwin's theory of evolution and how the weakest always survived because the stronger individuals of any species were off fighting and killing each other."

I raised an eyebrow at him, and Abigail chuckled. I didn't think she knew about the theory of evolution or why it was wrong, but she knew enough about her brother to tell from his tone that he was messing with me. She wanted in on the game.

"Yeah, and I'm learning about how when water evaporates, it turns into ice." She smiled.

"Ha-ha, guys. Very funny." It hadn't been so long since I was their age. I'd give them a pass on messing with me. It was like messing with the substitute teacher—kids just had to test their boundaries. "If that's what you're learning, I think I'll have to talk with your teachers directly. Seems like they're telling you some very incorrect things."

"No!" Abigail nearly shouted from her chair. "Don't talk to them!"

"Ah, okay, so do you maybe want to correct what you've told me?" I asked.

"Yes. Water turns into ice from freezing," she corrected.

I looked over at Drew, who said nothing. I could see he was still in the mood to challenge me.

He wasn't as young and easily scared as Abigail was.

"Very good. Why exactly does water do that?" I asked.

I took the time catching up a bit and then had Abigail work on some math problems for homework as I turned my attention to Drew who was extremely reluctant to answer my questions.

Frankly, I wasn't prepared for him to challenge me this much. I'd barely slept last night; I was too worried about what a fool I'd made of myself with Edward. I wasn't prepared for all the sass he wanted to throw at me, and I feared I was coming off a little weak.

That wasn't what I wanted. I didn't want to feel intimidated by either of the kids. I wanted to feel in my element. That was hard when I wasn't even convinced, I was fully qualified for this job, and I continued to make an ass out of myself at every opportunity.

Hell, I really wasn't qualified, was I? I only got the job because Edward made the argument that my lack of knowledge on the royal family was actually a

71

good thing for a tutor of the children. I wasn't so sure I agreed with him on that front.

I was relieved when it came time to take the kids to their riding lessons. Though Drew, once again, challenged me by telling me that he wasn't finished reading this chapter yet.

"Okay, well, you have to be done because it's time to go. We can't be late," I told him.

"One second," he groaned.

I ignored this and slammed the book shut in front of him. He looked up at me with frustration in his eyes, then turned around and marched out of the room angrily.

Abigail laughed at this too. "He hates the horses," she informed me.

"Really?" This surprised me.

"Yeah, he's not good at horseback riding like I am," she said proudly. "He'd rather be reading."

On that front, I could relate to Drew. I had never been too good at physical activities either. I was always a bookworm. I never even got particularly good at riding a bike.

Funny that I felt I could relate so strongly to Drew, but he resisted me so much.

I took the kids to their riding lessons, and even though I wanted to watch them on the horses, I decided against staying because I knew Drew probably wouldn't be too happy to see me. I went to the dining quarters again, where I ran into Millie.

"Hey, girl! How's your second day?" she said with a smile before she sipped her water.

"Not so well," I admitted. Again, I spoke to her as if we were long-term friends, because it felt that way.

"Uh-oh. You figured out who Edward is, huh?" She cringed.

I could feel myself blushing with embarrassment. "I discovered that last night, actually when the butler greeted him properly. He could have told me himself to save me the embarrassment. Oh, man, could I be a bigger idiot?"

"Hey, you're American. The royal family hasn't been drilled into your brain since you were old enough to talk."

73

"I'm an American working for the royal family! I should've done my research. I did do some research on the kids once I'd found out that I'd be working with them. I just didn't look too far into any of the other family members. Big mistake. Now I'm wondering if I'm going to lose my job for it."

"Nah, I don't think you will. The prince isn't really like that. He doesn't seem to take an interest in any of the staff, so he won't be bothered to talk to the queen about you. He can't be bothered with anything really."

"How do you mean?" I asked.

"He's very … well, let's just say he's not known to be the most responsible royal. He spends a lot of his time vacationing, meeting rich and beautiful women. He only pays attention to a few of his duties as prince, and that seems to only be when the queen or Ms. Mitchell are chiding him for his absences. He couldn't care less."

Huh… I hadn't known that, but it explained why he was so willing to shamelessly flirt with me.

"Well, even so, he might take a vested interest

in having me fired," I told her.

She raised an eyebrow. "Why do you think that?"

"Because I kind of … blatantly and rudely rejected him."

Her eyes widened. "No! You didn't!"

"Oh, yes, I most definitely did."

"He hit on you?" She seemed stunned.

"Yeah, totally. He asked me out last night."

"You said no?" She laughed. "But he's so ridiculously hot."

She was right about that; I couldn't deny it. I'd thought it from the first time I'd seen him. He was certainly handsome.

"I'm just not in a place for a relationship right now. With my dad being sick and trying to balance this new job, I have no interest in dating."

If I did have an interest…

Well, no… I couldn't date him now that I knew he was my boss. No matter how attractive he was.

"Well, if he hit on you, he knows that makes him looks bad," Millie pointed out. "I doubt he would ever tell anyone about it, let alone try to get you fired. I mean, that would be sexual harassment. He wouldn't do that."

Huh. Yeah, I was too busy with my stress to really think of it that way.

"I suppose you're right," I told her.

"So relax! Your job isn't in danger." She smiled sweetly.

"Unfortunately, that's not the only thing I'm stressed out about right now," I admitted.

"Oh? What else?" she asked.

"Well, I don't think the kids are taking me too well. Particularly Drew. He's challenging me at every opportunity, and I'm starting to doubt that I'm up to the task."

Millie looked at me sympathetically as she tucked her hair behind her ears. "I'm sure that you are, though. The thing is, those kids are going to challenge anyone who comes in here and tries to be the boss of them. All kids do that, but these kids especially. They have so many adults constantly telling them what to do, they're bound to rebel a bit."

"So, what should I do?" I asked. "I honestly don't want to be just another adult these kids have to rebel against."

"So don't be!" Millie suggested. "They're so used to stuffy, uptight authority figures. Maybe just be the person in their lives who is a little more relaxed? You know, don't let them walk all over you, but relate to them on their level. You don't have to be a Ms. Mitchell type. I don't even get the vibe that you like being an authority figure that much."

"I don't," I admitted. "I never have."

"So maybe the problem is that you're forcing yourself into a role you don't fit in, and the kids sense that weakness. Just be yourself. Reach them how you know how to reach them. Fill the role that actually feels natural."

Huh. I actually liked the idea of that. I had no desire to be another stuffy adult in their life anyway.

"That's genius. Thank you, Millie," I told her.

She seemed pleased with herself. "No problem at all. Now what to do about your prince problem?" she teased.

"Oh, I don't think that'll be a problem any longer. No way is he going to ask me out again after what a bitch I was."

Which was a good thing, right? Because I didn't want to date. I didn't want to have anything to do with him.

At least, that was what I told myself. In the back of my mind, I felt the slightest disappointment when thinking about Edward never wanting to speak to me again.

I left my dinner break a little early to catch the end of the kids' horseback riding lessons. I wanted the opportunity to talk to them again before I had to speak with their teachers.

Outside, I could see even from a distance that Abigail was a natural. She was trotting around the track like an absolute pro.

Whereas Drew's horse seemed to be just barely moving. As I got closer, I could see Drew nervously holding the reigns. Abigail was right—he clearly hated riding.

He saw me watching them, and I could see the

frustration on his face. Clearly, he'd rather I not be here. Maybe it was a mistake to come.

I wasn't going to walk away yet. Not until they finished and I had the chance to try my new technique on them.

They finished up the lesson, and the trainer helped them take the horses to the stables. It was Abigail who came sprinting out of the stables first, a grin plastered across her face.

"Did you see me?" she asked excitedly. "Did you see how good I was?"

I had to laugh at her confidence. I hoped she would never lose that. Confidence tended to be beaten out of you as you aged.

"I did! You were amazing. A real pro."

"My horse loves me!" she said as she skipped forward along the path.

Drew came out behind her, looking considerably less enthused. He tried to ignore me as he passed by.

"Hey, Drew. What's wrong?" I asked.

He looked at me, frustrated. "I'm no good. I've

79

been learning for years… I'm just no good at this."
He waved his hand at the stables.

"Hey, that's not a big deal," I told him. "You know, you don't have to be good at everything."

"I do," he said disappointedly. "My brother, Edward, is good at everything. He's going to be king. I could probably never be king… I can't even ride a horse."

"Hey, there! A king doesn't have to ride a horse." I put a gentle hand on his shoulder. "Drew, I promise you, there were a lot of things your brother wasn't good at when he was your age. It's just that he's older, and he's had more time to learn, so it looks like he's an expert at everything. I promise, he's not. Nobody is."

He looked at me curiously. "Not you either?"

I had to laugh. "Of course not, me either! Especially not me. There are so many things I'm bad at, I can't even count them, there's a lot of things I'm good at too. Like reading and learning. That's why I work as your tutor. I do the things I'm good at in life because it makes me happier than focusing on all the bad."

He seemed to understand this. "I'm pretty good at reading too."

"Yeah, you definitely are. I'm really impressed with how knowledgeable you are."

He smiled at hearing this, and I nudged his shoulder playfully. "I bet Edward wasn't such a good reader when he was your age."

He seemed contented with this. I felt more at ease. Millie was right. These kids had enough authority figures in their lives. I wanted to be someone they could talk to, someone they enjoyed learning from.

I'd be happier in that position more than anything else. I had a feeling the kids were going to be happier for it too

MCKENNA JAMES

Chapter 6

Edward

I found my younger sister nearly hopping along the hallways, looking positively delighted.

I narrowed my eyes at her. "What's gotten into you, Abby?"

"Miss Maggie said that today we get to have our lessons outside!" She told me happily. "I can't wait until she gets here!"

Ah, yes. Maggie… Of course, when I finally get the woman out of my head, my little sister had to bring her up.

"Outside? Really?" I asked.

This was odd to me. In all my lessons at the castle growing up, I'd never done any of them outside. It seemed pretty unorthodox, but it was interesting.

"Yeah! She said it'll be better if we learn outside today. I don't know why."

Drew came down the hall after her, his books in his hands.

While Abigail was entirely enthralled to be having lessons outside, I had a feeling that Drew was dreading it. If Abigail loved Maggie as a tutor, Drew probably hated her.

That was usually how it went anyway. Abigail and Drew got along just fine, but they were complete opposites. Anything Abigail loved, Drew hated, and vice versa.

I'd known him to be pretty hard on his teachers and tutors. He had a penchant for learning and had high standards for anyone teaching him.

"So how do you feel about the new tutor?" I asked.

"She's really nice." He smiled, to my surprise.

"Uh, really? You like her?"

"Yeah. She seems smart. She explains things really well. Especially for Abigail. She's even got Abigail to pay attention during lessons."

"And you don't mind going outside for lessons today?"

"Not at all. I'm sure if Maggie wants us outside, it'll be educational."

Wow, this was impressive. A tutor that both my brother and sister liked. Maybe my instincts weren't off about this one. She must have been something special if both my siblings were happy with her.

"Well, that's good. I'm glad you guys are happy with her," I told them as I made my way down the hall.

"Edward, want to come with us outside?" Abigail smiled at me.

She was a sweetheart, and she was always eager to spend more time with me. Both of my siblings were really, and I did enjoy my time with them. I knew so well the difficulty they experienced growing up as royals, and I wanted to alleviate that for them in any way that I could.

I didn't think it would be appropriate for me to spend time with them right now when they were going to be with Maggie. I had every intention of trying to pursue her in the future, but I wasn't going to do that in front of my siblings. I needed to smooth over the rejection first and win her over. It would take some charm, but I was a prince after all.

"I'm not so sure that's the best idea," I told Abigail.

"What's not the best idea?" I heard a soft voice say from behind me.

I turned around to see Maggie standing there, looking at me curiously.

"I asked Edward if he wanted to come out with us this afternoon!" Abigail gleamed.

"I was just about to say that I didn't think I should be interrupting any lessons." I smiled politely at Maggie.

The last time I'd seen her, she had been looking thoroughly embarrassed after discovering I was the prince. I wondered if she still felt any humiliation over that moment.

"You won't be interrupting," Abigail said. "Right, Maggie?"

Maggie forced a smile. "Right, of course not. You're welcome to join us."

I didn't think this invitation seemed genuine. It

felt as though she was only saying so to be polite, knowing that I was essentially now her boss. I doubted she actually wanted me there.

I couldn't resist her welcoming me, though. Looking at her again now, it was easy to see why I'd been struggling to get her out of my head. Man, she was gorgeous.

"Sure, alright. I'll tag along then."

"Yay!" Abigail cheered.

Maggie looked a tense.

I understood this. Even if I hadn't been rejected by her, and even if she hadn't realized I was the prince, it was hard to do your job with your boss standing over your shoulder.

I wasn't her boss, though. If anything, Ms. Mitchell was her boss. I may have hired her, but I had little interest in bossing her around.

"Well, let's head out then. I brought us some snacks." Maggie held up a picnic basket that she had hidden behind her back.

That was really sweet of her. Initially, I wanted to hire her because I was intrigued by her. I was glad she actually seemed to take a vested interest in this position.

We went out to the courtyard where Maggie spread out a large red blanket in the grass. She pulled out some simple snacks: crackers, cheese, yogurt, some juices. She moved to hand me a juice box, but I waved her off.

"I'm fine."

She took one for herself, though, which I thought was cute. I watched her sip that juice box and imagined her slurping on something much different...

No, stop it, Edward. Don't you dare think about anything gross when you're out here with your kid siblings and their tutor. I needed to behave as an adult. I was only here to spend time with my siblings.

"So I brought you guys outside today for two lessons. Let's do Abigail's first. Abigail, remind me and Drew of what you're learning about in science this week."

"We're learning about, uh..." Abigail trailed off with her thought.

88

"About the plants, right?" Maggie encouraged.

"Oh, yeah! About photosynthesis."

"Right. So I thought we'd take a walk around the rose gardens and talk about some of the plants that get their food by photosynthesis… instead of yogurt." She held up her cup.

Both Abigail and Drew had a chuckle.

"See all this green grass in front of us? Really pretty color, right, Abby?"

"Right!" Abigail agreed.

"What is the reason that it's all so green?"

"Chlorophyll!" Abigail said proudly.

"That's right. That's why so much of the beautiful nature we get to enjoy is so lush and green. Without chlorophyll, the world would definitely look like a much drabber place."

It was adorable watching her with the kids. I could tell that she actually cared about them. If this was just a job to her, she could be quizzing Abby on words like photosynthesis and chlorophyll indoors. She was actually going out of her way to instill in Abigail a love of learning, a reason to care about the

89

concepts she had been taught about in her science class.

I sat back quietly as I watched the rest of the lesson. She engaged both Abigail and Drew, and they were so enthralled with her, they hardly noticed my presence. Which was saying something since my siblings usually wanted to spend time with me above all others.

I couldn't believe I was actually enjoying watching a child's tutoring lesson.

She went on from the photosynthesis, and then she turned her attention to Drew's work. They talked about the water molecule for a while as I stared into her eyes and thought about how they were the familiar blue of the ocean. Of course, this quickly turned into thoughts of her on the beach in a bikini... I reminded myself again to snap back to reality.

"I don't get it," Drew said suddenly.

"Don't get what?" Maggie asked.

"You said that we had to be outside for both me and Abby's lessons today. Why did we need to learn about water outside?"

"Oh, uh, well…" Maggie looked at me hesitantly.

"What?" I asked. "What is it?"

"It's just… I kind of planned something, but I'm not sure it's appropriate now that you're here. And, uh, dressed so nicely."

I looked down at my clothes. I thought my outfit was fairly simple today, but evidently not.

"Well, I definitely don't want to interrupt the lesson. You should continue with whatever you had planned."

"Are you sure?" Maggie asked me skeptically.

"Yeah, I'm positive. Go for it."

"Okay…" She still seemed hesitant as she stood and walked away from the blanket.

Drew looked over at me with curiosity in his eyes. "Where is she going?"

"I don't know." I shrugged.

She walked over to a nearby shrub, and from behind it, she pulled out a very large bucket that looked like it was full of … balloons?

No, not just balloons—water balloons.

She grabbed one and threw it toward Abigail. It landed next to her with a splash, and she burst into laughter as both she and Drew eagerly walked over to the bucket to grab balloons.

I couldn't help but grin watching them. It was so simple, so childish, and it made my brother and sister so happy.

Abigail ran up to me and viciously threw a water balloon right at my chest. It burst on my shirt and soaked through it instantly.

"Oh, no, no, you do not want me to get into this fight," I threatened as I hopped to my feet and ran to the bucket.

I threw one at Abby, and then Maggie hit me in the chest again. I nailed her back, getting her shirt soaking wet.

The fabric clung to her, and I tried to keep myself from staring at the amazing curves of her body. I did my best to focus on the epic fight instead.

We were all laughing, soaked, when Drew suggested to Abby that they go try to get the gardeners with the balloons. Abigail naturally loved this idea and off they ran, leaving Maggie and I alone.

I smiled at her as I began to unbutton my sopping wet shirt.

"That was really sweet, you know," I said. "I don't think they have a lot of fun like that. I can tell they really love spending time with you."

This made her smile. "I love spending time with them too. They're really great kids."

As I peeled my shirt away from my skin, I could swear I saw her staring at my abs. Not to be too cocky, but I did spend a fair amount of time working out.

I stared at her back, letting my eyes actually linger on her torso. She didn't seem to mind, so I moved closer and turned my gaze directly toward her eyes.

"You know, I think wet clothes suit you…"

"Yeah?" she asked expectantly, moving closer to me too.

I was about to turn my head to kiss her, but before I could, Drew and Abigail came running back.

"We totally got them!" Drew said excitedly.

"I think Mr. Hansen was pretty mad, though!" Abigail chuckled.

I couldn't focus on their words at all. Instead, I was focused on my raging desire for Maggie.

I had to have her.

Whatever it took, I was going to find a way to have Maggie all to myself one of these evenings.

Chapter 7

Maggie

It had been a few weeks since I started working with Drew and Abigail, and I was loving every second of it. Not only was I less stressed about money and dealing with my father's hospital bills, but I'd really connected with the kids and was excited to go to work every day.

In a way, work had actually become my escape. Not that I didn't love spending time with my dad at home—of course, I did. I treasured every moment we had together. All those moments were certainly a stark reminder that he was ill and that I didn't know how much time we had left together.

Being with the kids was just a simple relief. With them, I could forget about the stresses of my father being ill and just enjoy our time together. They had both become so eager to learn. I had expected it from Drew, but even Abigail had a new zest for knowledge.

The only real downside to this job was Edward.

Okay, he wasn't a downside per se. I actually really enjoyed the time I spent with him, but that was kind of part of the problem. I had become enthralled with the man, and the last thing I needed was to become interested in any man. I definitely didn't want to be interested in my boss, of all people.

I did everything I could to avoid him, but he stopped in on our tutoring lessons fairly often. Every time he walked into the room; I could feel my heartbeat speed up. I hadn't felt like that since I had my first major crush in high school. Something about him just sent my head spinning.

I didn't know if it was his good looks or his devil-may-care attitude. he intrigued me. I was simultaneously desperate to learn more about him and eager to get as far away from him as I possibly could.

Which wasn't far since he lived at the castle as well, or so I assumed.

He hadn't asked me out since I rejected him, which was both a relief and a disappointment. As much as I knew rationally to stay away, I wanted him to press my boundaries and push for more. I wanted to explore with him.

Maybe I'd been too harsh in my initial rejection of him. Perhaps he didn't want to push boundaries lest it come off as sexual harassment. Or hell, maybe hiss attraction to me had worn off after spending countless hours with me and the children during tutoring.

I didn't really think that was the case, though. I could see the way he looked at me. He felt the same way I did—I could sense it.

Even though it made no damn sense to me at all. I mean, the man was a freaking prince, and who was I? Nobody. Some unknown American girl who struggled to make ends meet and spent her Friday nights taking care of her father. I wasn't his type. I wasn't rich, entertaining, and I could never go on crazy, elaborate vacations with him.

For some reason, that hadn't changed his mind. He still wanted me. Which I was grateful for.

And simultaneously worried about.

I heard a knock on the door and expected it to be Ms. Mitchell.

"Come in," I called out.

It wasn't Ms. Mitchell; instead, it was Edward.

"Sorry to interrupt," he said as he stepped through the door.

"Oh, no, you're not interrupting at all!" I answered, more eagerly than I intended to.

"I just wanted to stop by and ask if you'd like me to accompany you to the royal educational dinner tonight."

"Uh…" I furrowed my brow. "The … what now?"

"The royal educational dinner. Didn't they tell you?"

"I'm pretty positive they did not. What exactly is that?"

"It's an annual dinner we host for all the members of our educational staff. It's tonight. You should have received your invitation and outfit. Wait, hold on…" He pulled out his phone. "You do live in the Wayfield Flats … number 67?"

"Uh, no… Number 76."

"Ah, well, I guess we figured out the problem. I'll make sure they deliver a dress to the correct address this time. It should arrive by seven this evening, just in time for you to make the eight o'clock dinner."

"I … don't think that will be necessary," I told him. "I'm busy tonight. Actually, I'm busy most nights. I have prior responsibilities."

Edward tightened his lips. "I'm afraid you don't really have a choice. It's a requirement for your position. All our educators must attend."

Great. I'd have to ask my dad's caregiver if she'd be willing to work overtime tonight.

"Then I suppose I'll be there," I said, defeated.

"Terrific. Then I'll have you as my date. I will have my driver arrive at your home at 7:30."

"Now wait a second…" I began to say.

I was going to tell him I hadn't necessarily agreed to be his date, but he had already left the room. He wasn't going to take no for an answer.

I sighed and looked over at Abigail and Drew. "Your brother … he's quite determined, isn't he?"

"Mom says Edward always gets what he wants," Abigail said as if she was telling me a dirty secret.

"Well, I can certainly believe that."

***

When I went home that evening, a dress was indeed waiting for me. It was hanging on the inside of my door; my dad's caregiver must have brought it in. She agreed to work late for me after I explained the obligation. My dad wasn't even awake for me to tell him of the plan for the night.

I pulled the dress out of its plastic packaging and was stunned by how beautiful it was. Perhaps I shouldn't have been … it was for a royal event after all.

It was a full-length, midnight blue gown that was dusted with gold sparkles. After doing my hair and makeup, I slid into it and was almost unrecognizable from myself. I hadn't been this dolled up in … well, never. I'd never worn anything quite this fancy.

It felt silly walking out of my flat in this extravagant gown and high heels. I looked around anxiously, hoping that nobody would catch me on the way to the car.

Which was impressively nice. I didn't know much about cars, but the door lifted up instead of out. Edward was standing outside the car to let me in, even though there didn't appear to be much for him to do.

"Thank you," I said politely, and as I slid myself into the back seat, the door slowly slid into place.

Edward walked around the car and got in next to me. He looked as handsome as ever. I tried not to get too swept up in the magic of the moment. I mean, attending a royal event with the Prince of England was like something out of a romantic comedy.

I sure didn't have a romantic comedy kind of life.

"So what responsibilities would you normally have on a Friday night?" Edward asked, seemingly out of nowhere.

"Huh?" I said.

"When I first informed you of the dinner, you said you had other responsibilities to tend to. What were those?"

"Oh, uh…" For a moment, I considered coming up with a lie because speaking about my father right now felt heavy. For some reason, looking into his eyes, I felt compelled to tell the truth.

"My father has cancer, and he needs me around. I have a caregiver for when I'm at work, but when she's not around, I try not to leave him alone for more than an hour or so."

He looked stunned by this. "Oh, wow. I had no idea… Maggie, I'm so sorry. Your mother…" he suddenly trailed off, seemingly nervous to finish his inquiry.

"She died a few years ago of breast cancer. I sort of escaped my life for a while by coming to university here in London, but when my dad fell ill…" I looked away as I tried to control the emotions. I didn't like to talk about my parents and their illnesses. It was like pouring salt into an open wound—painful, no matter the time that had passed.

"You're a very strong young woman to have overcome such tragedies." He grasped my hand and squeezed, extending his strength to me. I appreciated that.

I smiled at him. "Don't be. That's life, right? Things pop up, you end up taking more responsibility than you wanted to, but you do what you have to do. I love my father, and now that I have a better paying job, I'm less stressed about money. So, it's all working out."

He nodded.

"I'm sure you have to do a lot of things you never wanted to as prince, right?" I asked, mostly eager to change the subject.

"Well no, not really. I mean, there are a lot of things I should be doing that I don't want to do, but I mostly get to shirk my responsibilities at every given opportunity."

I laughed. "You know, I'd heard something like that around the palace."

"What's that? That I'm an entirely irresponsible man-child?" He took it in stride.

"Something like that."

He laughed. "I can be, I'll admit it. I'm only going to be young once. One day I'll actually be king and have to deal with all the responsibilities that come with that. I need to have fun while I still can."

"So, you don't want to be king?" I asked.

"Of course not," he scoffed. "What child grows up wanting to be king?"

"Um, I think a better question is what child doesn't grow up wanting to be king?" I laughed.

He thought on this a moment. "Okay, admittedly, I might have a different perspective growing up as royalty. I never wanted it. In fact, I grew up wishing that I was a normal kid. I wanted to go to school like normal kids and make regular friends and make mistakes and just live my life. I hated that cameras followed us on every vacation and that I could hardly leave the palace. I did everything I could to rebel against it because I didn't want it. When I was finally shipped off to a boujie boarding school in high school, I was relieved to finally have some freedom. I suppose I really took that freedom and ran it was about the only thing that had ever made me happy in the slightest."

I nodded. "I mean, it makes sense. I'd probably be the same way. It's easy to fantasize about fame before you ever have to actually deal with it."

"Right," he agreed. "As I watch Drew and Abigail grow up, I'm reminded of how messed up it can be. They're so isolated from the world. I'm glad they at least have you, someone to be normal with them."

I smiled hearing this. That was exactly what I wanted to provide for those kids, and I was relieved to know that in some small way, I had made their lives more normal.

We arrived at the dinner shortly thereafter, and he acted like a perfect gentleman. He buckled arms with mine as we walked into the palace dining hall, which was set with an elaborate feast on a long mahogany table. I recognized many of Abigail and Drew's teachers, but there were a few people I did not recognize.

When I saw the queen seated at the head of the

table, my heart almost dropped. Suddenly I was worried that it would seem inappropriate for me to have come with Edward. I was an employee, after all, and I probably shouldn't be fraternizing with royalty.

If anyone was going to get in trouble for that, I imagined it would be Edward. He was the one who had the responsibility to not date the staff.

We took our seats, and I kept a smile plastered on my face, hoping it would look like I fit in. I didn't feel as if I fit in, though. I felt completely out of place. In fact, my entire life was beginning to feel out of place.

I mean, what on earth was I doing here with the prince? I wasn't the kind of woman he should be with. Why did he even have an interest in me?

I tried not to dwell on it. The more I did, the more my social anxiety kicked in. I was already so anxious... If I let myself overthink anymore, I wasn't going to be able to talk to anybody.

Fortunately, it didn't seem like anyone was particularly interested in talking to me. The educators mostly talked amongst themselves. I was just a tutor.

I wasn't important enough for them to speak to at a royal dinner.

The only one who seemed interested in talking to me was Edward. He did talk to me, at length.

"Let's break the tensions right from the start. I can see you worrying your lip." Edward grasped my hand in his and pulled me up from the chair, keeping my fingers laced in his.

"What are you doing?"

"I'm introducing you to my mother," he called back over his shoulder, and I immediately dug my heels into the ground.

"Oh no you're not!" Edward boomeranged back toward me and chuckled to himself, looking back over his shoulder to toss a wayward greeting to a couple passing by.

"What is there to be nervous about, Maggie? You're an employ to the crown. You work closely with her youngest children each day, and you're working your way into my life despite my continuous rejections." He laughed playfully, releasing the anxiety that had suddenly consumed me. I felt safe and carefree with Edward, so I decided to allow him this one request.

"Okay, Prince Edward, I'm graciously prepared to meet the queen." I mock curtsied to lighten the mood.

"Showoff. Come, right this way."

As we made our way toward the queen's position at the head of the royal table, I was in a fog. With each step I took, I was oblivious to my surroundings, and my hands began to sweat as my nerves ramped up. I felt a sudden bump and looked up to realize Edward has stopped suddenly and I'd crashed into his back.

"You must calm down, Maggie. No need for fear or anxiety. The queen herself will tell you, she is but an everyday woman, much like you, only with the responsibility of millions upon her shoulders."

I nodded as I blinked rapidly, trying to clear the fog.

"Are you ready, because there's no turning back now."

"Mother, I'd like to introduce you to Abigail

108

and Drew's tutor, Miss Maggie Spencer."

Before I knew it, I was curtsying before the queen, my tongue lodged in my throat as I tried to coerce the words out. This moment—it was far more exciting than realizing I'd just spilled scalding hot coffee down the Prince of England's chest.

"Your highness, it is my honor to stand in your presence," I bowed my head in respect of the Queen.

"Hello, my dear. It's a pleasure to make your acquaintance."

The Queen motioned to the chairs adjacent to her position. "Please, have a seat and tell me about yourself."

I looked at Edward in shock as he pulled the chair away from the table for me. I sat, placing my hands in my lap nervously. "We-well, as Prince Edward mentioned, I'm the new tutor for Prince Drew and Princess Abigail, who are simply delightful children. It's a true honor to play a small part in their enrichment."

"We are very appreciative of your dedication

as tutor. Will you eventually seek a position in teaching?"

I shook my head, ashamed to admit my education was short-lived. "No definite plans, Your Highness, but a girl can dream that eventually I may be lucky enough to complete my degree."

"Maggie ended her studies at the university earlier than intended to care for her ailing father."

"My, how noble of you. I hate to hear that your father is ill."

It amazed me how easy it was to carry on a conversation with the Queen of England. Her dignified demeanor melted away as we spoke about everything from my role as tutor for the children to Prince Edward's newfound friend, only to be interrupted by the announcement that dinner was being served. Edward and I said goodbye to his mother as he escorted me back to our places at the table.

"So how does it feel to be here tonight?" he asked as we ate.

"Honestly, it was a little awkward at first," I admitted. "Meeting your mother was the highlight of the night, but I honestly feel out of place. I'm not sure how I'm supposed to behave exactly."

"That's normal," he assured me. "I still feel that way after all these years."

"How do you feel about fame now?" I asked, turning the attention off of me.

"Huh?" He turned to me, confused.

"Well, you said while growing up, fame was hard, but how do you feel about it now? Surely it has its advantages, at least."

"I don't think it does," he answered, then taking a drink of wine. "Unless you consider never knowing someone's true intentions an advantage. I'm one of the most popular young men in all of London, and yet, I'm desperately lonely. I don't know if I can name even one true friend I have."

Well, that was depressing to think about. I never considered that aspect of it. Even adults who become famous through a singing or acting career were at one time normal people, and they were able to make friends under normal circumstances.

Edward never got to do that. He had always

been this famous, even as an infant.

"People are constantly flocking to me because they want my fame or they want my money. The sad thing is that most of the time, I let them because, well, I'd be on my own entirely if I didn't let people use me to their advantage. I'll do just about anything to curb the loneliness."

"Wow," I muttered. "I'm so sorry. That truly does sound horrible. I can't imagine, always being surrounded by people who don't have your best interests at heart."

He sighed. "It's difficult, to say the least. I think that's why I took such an interest in you."

I didn't follow. "Why, exactly?"

"Because interacting with you was the first time I ever interacted with someone who had no idea who I was. What you had said to me was entirely genuine, if not occasionally harsh."

I laughed. "Sorry. I could've been less cold when you asked me out. It wasn't you. I mean, you seem like a nice guy, and I'm sure I don't need to tell you how handsome you are either. There are several reasons why I felt it best to keep my distance, and your playboy persona was one, to be honest. Really, I'm just not looking to date. With everything going on with my father, I couldn't give anyone my full attention."

He looked at me and smiled. "What if it's not your full attention I want?"

"Um, how do you mean?" I asked.

"I mean, we're both adults here. We can be forthcoming with each other. What if I don't want your full attention? What if I just want ... one night?"

I was both shocked by how blunt he was and intrigued by it. This man really had no shame, huh?

I wanted to reject him just to do it, just to show him that I wasn't easy. Then again, why should I? What would that prove? Did I need to show him my virtue? Why should I care what he thought of me?

I didn't care. It had been so very long since I'd had any fun with anyone.

I couldn't date—wouldn't date—but really, what would be the harm in a one-night stand? I mean, it would always make for a pretty damn good story.

A one-night stand with the Prince of England?

I smiled at him. "You really think you could handle just one night with me? One night and that's it?"

"The real question is going to be whether or not you can handle me."

That sent a shiver down my spine.

"So after dinner … my place?" He grinned.

"Wait, you have your own place? Like, outside the palace?"

"Of course I do! You didn't think I'd let myself be stuck here all the time, did you? No, I could never. I have a penthouse in downtown London. Would you care to visit it with me?"

My heart pounded out of my chest as I tried to decide how to answer. I didn't want to say yes. I didn't want to give in to my primal desire for him.

I didn't want to pass up the opportunity to actually enjoy myself for a night. After all that I'd been through recently, didn't I deserve that?

I nodded.

"Perfect." He grinned, clearly pleased with

himself.

The five-course meal was the longest of my life. Though the food was absolutely decadent, and I was a girl who loved to eat, I couldn't really enjoy any of it. It wasn't food I was hungry for anymore—it was Edward. I was eager to get back to his place.

Though I felt guilty thinking about that with the queen on the far end of the table.

Ah, well, I couldn't control my desires. It'd been a long time, and Edward was absolutely gorgeous. Not to mention that I'd really come around to his attitude. Yes, he was a bit arrogant, but he was also very warm. He'd been a charming gentleman all evening—exactly what you'd expect from a prince. I'd thoroughly enjoyed myself with him; but the night was still young.

Though my desire for idle chatter had all but dissipated.

When the dinner was finally done, we snuck away rather quickly, and Edward had his driver take us to his penthouse.

The car ride there was a bit awkward, not at all

filled with the same conversation we had had previously. I was too nervous to talk. It'd been so long since I'd been with a man, I was worried that I might not … be up to par, so to speak.

I wondered what was keeping Edward so quiet, though. Surely it wasn't nervousness. He must have done this all the time with random women. I highly doubted he was getting nervous or bothered over little old me.

When we arrived at his penthouse, I only became jumpier.

It was one thing to not fit in at the palace. I felt as though I didn't belong, but at least I knew that I really was supposed to be there as a requirement of my job.

It was entirely different walking into the lobby of his penthouse where a doorman let us in. He even opened the elevator door for us, as if we needed another person just to push a button.

This was a level of elite I wasn't made for. And I was starting to regret my decision to come when we reached the inside of his penthouse.

Which was absolutely, positively, stunning.

It was the exact opposite of the palace and yet no less elegant. The palace had a very classic feel to it. The penthouse, by contrast, was entirely modern. It was clearly a rebellion on Edward's part.

"Your place is beautiful," I said softly.

"Thank you." He smiled. "Nowhere near as beautiful as you."

MCKENNA JAMES

Chapter 8

Edward

She was positively stunning. I couldn't peel my eyes away. I watched carefully as she glanced around my penthouse. She seemed amazed by it but not as enthralled as I was by her.

I was ravenous for her. I loved the way her curvy body looked in that dress. It hugged her in all the right places. It took everything I had not to take a bite out of her tight ass.

I was normally quite good at making a first move. I had a confidence about me. I knew that women often wanted me, and I exploited that when I could.

Something felt different tonight. I wasn't sure I could bring out that kind of confidence with Maggie. Something about her made me shrink back. I felt almost as though she was too good for me.

That wasn't going to be enough to keep me

from her, though. I just had to push aside my insecurities and go for it.

Normally, I would lean in and kiss her, tonight I decided to take a different approach.

"Would you like to accompany me to the bedroom?" It didn't come off as smooth as I had hoped, but she was still receptive.

"I would." She smiled.

I took her hand in mine and led her to the room. All the while, there was an eager pounding in my chest. I could already picture how gorgeous she was going to look after I had this dress peeled off of her body.

"Wow, every single room is just downright gorgeous," she marveled as she stepped inside.

I closed the door behind us and went to the fireplace.

"Glad you like it," I said as I started a fire. I was hoping it would set the mood.

Though she seemed skeptical of it.

"A fire? Isn't that a little romantic?" she asked.

"Don't you like a little romance before ... you

120

know?"

She laughed.

"Edward, I knew why I was coming here. If I wanted romance, I would've insisted you take me to a five-star establishment and woo me properly." I shook my head. "No, I don't want romance."

"So what is it you want?" I asked.

"I want a night of absolute fiery passion. I want you to make me scream so loud, the people below will hear me."

I tried to hold back my smile.

"That may be hard to do. This is an expensive place; the walls are thick."

"Then I hope you're up to the task."

She slowly began to unzip the side of her dress. I felt like I was nearly salivating as I watched her with my jaw dropped. She had a gorgeous silhouette, but it held nothing on her naked figure.

I watched as the sparkly blue dress fell to the floor. She stood before me in lacy black lingerie. I could see through it a bit. Still, I was desperate to get the whole show.

She stared at me. "You do know how this works, right? You see me, then I get to see you..."

God, I loved how sassy and confident she was. That wasn't something I was expecting. She normally came off so reserved.

It was always the quiet ones who were the wildest in bed.

I started to unbutton my shirt. I could see her ogling my abs as I dropped my pants.

I moved toward her, only in my boxers now. I wouldn't take them off until I got her panties off first.

I knelt before her, grabbing the side of her panties with my teeth and pulling them down. She gasped as I exposed her, the cool air kissing her skin.

I had my face against her bare pussy. It was beautiful. I wasn't sure I'd seen any woman as beautiful as her in a long time. That was saying something because I was practically surrounded by beautiful women on a daily basis.

I moved in closer to her, exposing my tongue to her clit. Again, she gasped, but this time she also dug her hands into my shoulders. I loved hearing her shocked pleasure and was determined to hear more.

I slid my tongue up and down her slit with her still standing. I moved slowly at first then began to increase my speed. I licked at her clit, rolling circles around it until she was properly moaning before exploring her crevice further.

I slid my hand down her pussy. I felt the outside at first, did my best to assess how wet she was and if she was ready for my fingers to enter her.

She felt soaked. I slid two fingers inside, and she screamed out.

"Oh, yes!" She tossed her head back.

I began to pump my fingers in and out of her. My cock tingled with every movement.

It wasn't long before her legs began to tremble. She couldn't continue to stand and take all the pleasure I was giving her.

I lifted her quickly, carrying her to my bed and then tossing her on top of it.

She began to unhook her bra, and I dropped my boxers. My cock was already standing at attention, she stared at it and then looked up at me.

"I want it. Now."

Well, I couldn't keep the woman waiting, could I?

I climbed on top of her, pushing both her legs back and exposing her tight pussy. I began to put the tip of my prick at her entrance and then slowly rocked myself into her.

Evidently, this wasn't what she wanted.

"No," she insisted, "hard!"

She was ready for me.

I slammed myself into her in one fell swoop. She screamed out as my balls slapped against her ass.

She was even tighter than I imagined. Her entire pussy was hugging my cock. Thankfully, she was so wet that it was effortless to glide in and out of her.

I put my hands on her wrists and pinned her down as I began to pound her ruthlessly. With every pump, her entire body was pushed upward. She didn't seem to mind. She was writhing under me, eager for anything that I could give her.

She was already so riled up from the oral that I thought she might come at any minute. I didn't want that. I knew that if she came, I might too. It would be too hot to watch her orgasm.

I slowed down a bit. I pulled my cock out nearly all the way then slammed back into her. I made focused thrusts in and out of her. She panted underneath me.

I stared at her body underneath me as I thrust into her. I loved the way every bit of her body jiggled. Her tits looked amazing as I drilled her. She was easily the most beautiful woman I'd ever been with.

"Faster, faster, I'm going to come!" she pleaded with me.

I couldn't deny her, even if I did want this to last longer. If she wanted a strong finish, I was damn well going to give her one.

I pounded at her viciously. She was screaming at the top of her lungs. I thought about her comment regarding my downstairs neighbor … now I realized it wasn't a joke.

I knew the exact moment she came. She made a guttural groan as her legs began to tremble underneath me, and I could feel her pulsating around my cock. It was as if she was milking me.

That was all that I could handle. Watching her pleasure pushed me over the edge, and I felt myself come into her. My balls tensed up and released as I shot rope after rope into her tight pussy.

When I'd finished, I pulled myself out and collapsed on the bed next to her.

We didn't say anything for a while. I took that to be a good thing. Generally, I liked to leave a woman both speechless and breathless. She seemed to still be catching hers as was I.

Eventually, she rolled over to face me. Even after just coming, I couldn't stop myself from being amazed by her naked body.

"That was truly fantastic," she whispered.

"For me too." I smiled at her.

"You are clearly, uh, very experienced with women…"

"I like to think so."

I didn't care if I sounded too full of myself. In that moment, I *was* full of myself. I'd just made the most beautiful woman I'd ever met orgasm. I was feeling damn good.

She stretched out a bit then sighed.

"I suppose I should get going."

"Wait? What? Why?" I asked, suddenly shocked.

"Well, I mean, we did do what I came here to do, right?"

She wasn't kidding when she said she didn't come here for romance.

This was unusual to me. I didn't usually sleep with women who were eager to run out the door. On the contrary, they usually overstayed their welcome, sleeping over and then wanting to eat breakfast the next morning.

Oddly enough, though, I wouldn't mind that with Maggie. Her presence really put me at ease. I was hoping she'd consider staying the night with me. She was someone I'd be happy to eat breakfast with the next day. Hell, I could even take her to work.

"I mean, you don't have to rush off or anything. I don't want you to feel like I'm pushing you out the door."

She sat up and then got off the bed.

"I don't feel that way," she assured me.

"Uh, okay, I guess. Really, feel free to stay as long as you want."

"Ahh … I see now." She grinned at me.

"What?" I asked, entirely clueless to her implication.

"You were hoping you'd be able to get in a round two tonight, huh?"

"No, I really was not—"

"Well, I hate to break it to you, but one mind-blowing orgasm is about all I can handle. But thank you. It was fantastic." She walked over to her dress and slipped it on.

Although, even clothed, all I could think of now was her naked body. I hoped that wasn't something that would continue. I didn't want to be eye-balling her as she worked.

"At least let my driver take you home?" I asked.

"No, no, it's fine. I'll get a car, I do it all the time."

She grabbed her cell phone and before I could protest anymore, it was clear that she had already requested a car.

"Okay, well … thank you for coming over."

"Of course. Bye, Edward."

"Bye, Maggie."

I listened intently as she walked away from my bedroom. With every step, I considered calling out to her, asking her to consider staying with me. I chickened out.

When I heard her open and shut my penthouse door, I was more than a little disappointed.

I sighed as I threw my hands behind my head and tried to process what had just happened.

I looked over at the other side of my bed and couldn't help but think about how nice it would be if Maggie was sleeping there.

I thought that sleeping with her would finally get her out of my system but evidently not.

Damn, I had it bad for this one.

MCKENNA JAMES

Chapter 9

Maggie

I woke up the next morning completely and utterly embarrassed.

I felt like I'd made a fool of myself the night before.

I couldn't say I necessarily regretted what had happened. The sex was phenomenal, and Edward was amazing.

I didn't expect for the sex to come with so many ... feelings.

If I thought that I was actually going to be attracted to Edward in a way that wasn't simply physical, I never would have done it. I should have known not to do it anyway. I'd never been great at separating sex from emotion.

I was especially bad at it with this man.

I was attached, and I knew it. Which meant everything we did was a really bad idea because, well, there was no way Prince Edward felt the same.

I wouldn't expect him to. He made his feelings very clear. We wanted a one-night stand. He was looking for some fun. Those were the conditions I'd agreed to. There was no going back on it in retrospect. I made the choice knowing that it was nothing serious.

Now I wished I hadn't made it.

I couldn't be Edward's fling. I had decided that already. If he ever wanted to hook up again then it was most certainly going to be a no. That much I knew.

Even so, I dreaded going back to work knowing I would have to see him. Just another reason that agreeing to have sex with him was an awful idea. He was basically my boss! I had to see him every day at work!

Work was, up until just recently, a sanctuary for me. I shouldn't have tainted it by getting too caught up in all my feelings.

Well, nothing I could do about it now. It wasn't as if I was going to quit. No way. This was my dream job. I just had to power through it for now and hope that Edward would move on quickly as well.

Actually, maybe he already had. I mean, he did make it seem like I was just this craving he wanted to get out of his system. We'd had sex, so maybe he'd done that.

That would be ideal because if he was over me, he'd leave me alone and let me do my job.

Even as I thought it, I hoped it wasn't true. It broke my heart to think that Edward could push me aside so quickly after having sex. I certainly couldn't do the same to him.

If he was able to push me aside, though, and if there was never going to be anything between us, then I'd rather be left alone. I was sure that in a few weeks I'd be over the whole thing, work would become my sanctuary again, and I could focus on the kids and not on Edward. As long as he let me be, this would all be fine.

***

I had decided to have an alternative lesson plan today. I'd called Ms. Mitchell and asked if I could get permission to take Abigail and Drew to the Museum of London. That way we could learn outside of the palace while also avoiding Edward. It seemed perfect.

Ms. Mitchell told me that she would have to run it by the Queen, and she wasn't sure because it was such short notice. Ultimately, she called back about forty-five minutes later to inform me that we could go to the museum and guards were on standby for our departure. Guards. That was something I still hadn't adapted to, but I understood the necessity for safety of the royals.

I didn't care who tagged along on our trip as long as it wasn't Edward.

The field trip served a double purpose for me. I was relieved that I wasn't going to have to see Edward today, and at the same time, I was distracted by how excited I was to tell the kids that we'd actually be going on a field trip. I knew Abigail would be delighted because she was always happy to go on any new adventure, and Drew would be excited because he loved museums. He loved anything that helped him gain knowledge. He was such a sweet boy.

I went into work feeling like I could handle the day. No Edward, a little joy with the kids … it was going to be alright.

I met the kids in our usual room with a smile on my face. Abigail immediately knew something was up.

"What? What is it?" she asked.

"Well, I've got something a little unusual planned for us today. I thought we could take our tutoring lesson over to the Museum of London. How would you guys feel about that?"

"Awesome!" Drew grinned.

"Okay, great! So, Ms. Mitchell has a ride arranged for us. Go ahead and leave all your books here, and we'll be on our way!"

Abigail slammed her books down onto the table before sprinting out of the room and down the stairs excitedly. Drew moved a lot slower, though he seemed no less excited.

I followed them downstairs, but when we

reached the bottom of the staircase, there was a fluttering in my stomach.

Edward was there, leaning against the banister and smiling at me.

"Hey there, Maggie."

"Oh, uh, hi. Sorry, no time too really talk right now … gotta get the kids to their lesson."

"We're going to the Museum of London!" Drew said excitedly.

"You are?" Edward gleamed. "Well, I happen to adore the Museum of London. Mind if I tag along?"

"Um … what?" I asked, stunned.

This wasn't how I was hoping this would go. I didn't even plan to see Edward today, and I certainly didn't anticipate that I'd have to be trapped in a car with him and subsequently stuck for an entire museum trip.

Well, this plan really backfired.

"I, uh—" I couldn't think of a good reason he shouldn't come.

"Yay! Edward is coming!" Abigail cheered.

136

Now I really couldn't turn him away.

Edward smiled. "Perfect! I'm excited to be tagging along."

I forced a smile, but it was entirely fake. I had a feeling Edward knew it too because he looked at me curiously.

If he knew I was uncomfortable, he wasn't going to let that stop him from coming along.

The car ride was, as I expected, sufficiently awkward. It did help that the kids were chattering nonstop. If it wasn't for them, there would have probably be a very uncomfortable silence.

I told myself that I could do this today, especially with the kids here. They'd create the conversation, and Edward and I would never truly be alone, which meant we would never have to talk about last night.

Though anytime he caught the children's attention elsewhere, Edward kept making eyes at me. I knew those eyes. He was giving me the 'I've seen you naked' eyes. I hated it.

He inched a closer to me in the car, his hand

brushing against my thigh. I reacted by moving further away from him. For a moment he seemed confused, then subsequently amused. I looked out the window instead of at him.

Things became a lot easier once we arrived at the museum. Ms. Mitchell had set us up with a guided tour, and two bodyguards were following us around the museum. It felt a bit crowded and certainly didn't leave any room for Edward to speak to me or ask me anything.

Just like Drew, I loved museums. I loved seeing history up close in front of me.

I loved the *London Before London* exhibit. Seeing this land before civilization had begun was so humbling to me. It was a reminder that I was so small, just a speck of dust in this planet's timeline, not even slightly important to the world.

This might bother some people, but it didn't bother me. In fact, I found it comforting. Within all of life's great stresses, I liked to know that nothing I did really mattered. Whatever was stressing me out, it was insignificant when you looked at the grand scheme of things. Knowing that took a lot of weight off of me.

"I have to go to the bathroom!" Abigail nearly shouted.

"I can take her!" Drew said eagerly. "I know where they are!"

I looked up at our guards, who both nodded.

"Okay, they'll take you both. We'll stay here," I told them.

They ran off to the restrooms, which, unfortunately, left me and Edward awkwardly alone.

"I enjoyed our evening, and I hated for it to come to an end," Edward said as he leaned closer into me.

I felt a chill go down my spine at his close proximity. I hated how much he affected me. I couldn't resist this man.

Which was why I wanted to stay away from him in the first place.

I pretended I didn't hear him. "Oh, what? Sorry. I'm just really fixated on this exhibit."

He looked at me curiously. "Have you ever

been to the Museum of London?"

"Just once before," I told him. "This exhibit was my favorite then too."

He didn't take his eyes off me. "Really? It kind of bothers me."

"Why?" I asked. "I'd think if anything it would really appeal to someone like you."

"How so?"

"Well, it's kind of a reminder to me that all of our decisions are pointless, really. We're so insignificant to the world, even more insignificant to the universe. It's a freeing thought."

"I don't find it freeing," he said as he turned toward the exhibit. "I find it anxiety-inducing. All my life I've been told I have this important role to play. That my decisions matter. Then I look at this, and it doesn't feel that way."

"Wouldn't you like that?" I asked. "I mean, you said you don't want that responsibility, don't want that weight. So, wouldn't you appreciate that weight feeling lifted?"

He looked at me curiously. "I hadn't thought

140

about it like that before."

I looked into his eyes, he looked into mine, and I felt our chemistry once again.

It was electric.

MCKENNA JAMES

Chapter 10

Edward

It was obvious to me that Maggie was avoiding me. In a way, I found it kind of cute. I was also very confused about why.

I thought we had a great time together. Although she did rush out a bit after we hooked up, I didn't give it much thought.

I had assumed that once I finally had her, I'd relax, and she wouldn't consume my thoughts so much. But the exact opposite had happened.

I thought of her even more now. I specifically came to the palace today just to see her, just to interact. So I was excited when I heard they were going to the museum. I thought it would be my opportunity to spend some time with her.

Now I could see that, for her, it was an opportunity to avoid me.

Still, I would not be deterred. I didn't know

why I still wanted to spend time with her, but I knew that nothing was going to stop me from doing so. I liked her, really liked her, and I would do whatever it took to keep seeing her.

I had never felt this way about a woman. There'd been plenty of women I'd dated, plenty of women I'd spent adequate time with whom I enjoyed. At the end of the day, I could take them or leave them. I didn't feel like I needed to spend significant time with any of them.

I needed to spend time with Maggie. Craved every moment that she was near.

"When you are dealing with the stresses associated with your father's illness, is this the kind of thinking that calms you?" I asked her, referring to the exhibit and the way it made her feel insignificant.

"Actually, yeah. When the medical bills were piling up and I wasn't sure if I'd be able to make it, when I thought of the rising debt and my credit score being ruined, I thought of how silly that all was. Money, debt, credit scores ... all things man made up to feel like they had some control over the world. We don't have control of the world at all, do we? It's always done as it pleased, and it always will."

I was so enthralled by her every word. She thought in a way that I never had before, though we did walk down two very different paths in life, and although I had no desire to struggle or feel the angst and suffering she'd spoke up, it gave me a newfound respect for her, for her family, for never giving up and working harder simply in the name of love.

Though I hated thinking about her struggle with her father. It didn't seem fair to me that someone like her should have to struggle so much. She was so kind, so smart, so wonderfully beautiful... I wished I could take away all of her hardships.

"The kids will be back any moment, you know," I told her.

"Can't wait." She smiled but said it bitingly. She was making it clear she didn't want to be alone with me.

Why? Perhaps she didn't trust herself in my presence.

"You don't enjoy spending time together?" I

145

asked.

"No, uh, I do…" she muttered.

"So … what is it then?"

"I'm just not so sure it's a good idea," she told me.

"Why not?"

She shrugged. "I don't know, it's just … you're my boss, you know?"

Oh, so that was what this was about.

"Maggie, I'm not your boss. Not really. Have I ever felt like a boss to you?"

"Not really…" she said quietly.

"Well, then, what's the harm?"

Before she could argue, I clasped her face within my hands and leaned in to kiss her. I wasn't sure if she'd pull away, but I had to risk rejection while the opportunity was present. She surprised me in the best way. The kiss was soft, gentle—romantic. Exactly what she promised she didn't want, didn't need. Completely opposite, however, where I was concerned.

She never pulled back, though. In fact, she put

her hand on my cheek as she leaned forward.

I savored the taste of her lips on my own. She was delicious... I had flashbacks of our night together.

Then, suddenly, she took her lips from mine.

"I, uh, don't want the kids to see," she muttered.

"Right," I agreed, not all that eager for my younger siblings to catch me making out with their tutor either. "Then meet me later tonight? After you finish work?"

"Like ... meet you at the palace? After work hours?"

"Yes," I said seriously.

She once again seemed hesitant. "I don't know... I'm not sure that's a good idea."

"Well, I am," I told her. "I'm positive it's a damn good idea. I want to see you again... No, I absolutely have to see you again."

Her eyes widened a bit. "You ... have to?"

"I insist," I repeated.

She sighed. "Okay ... sure. Yes, I'll meet you

later."

I smiled. "Perfect."

The timing was just right because only a moment later, I saw Abigail and Drew running toward us.

"Are you guys ready to get back on the tour?" Maggie asked.

"Yes!" Abigail answered excitedly.

I wasn't.

I couldn't focus on anything at the museum. The only thing I could focus on, the only thing I wanted to focus on, was Maggie. I found myself obsessively thinking about later when I would have her alone to myself again. Everything I might do to her when given the opportunity.

It had me thoroughly excited.

I pretty much zoned out for the rest of the tour. Abigail or Drew would occasionally engage me, and of course I'd answer, but then my mind would drift back to Maggie.

I watched her endlessly. I loved the way she moved. I loved her curvy body. I loved the way her hair bounced with every step … as well as her ass. As she walked, I imagined that body walking naked toward me.

I couldn't believe how insatiably I wanted this woman. I was not this guy. Why did I feel such strong desire to be around her? Why couldn't I get her out of my head? This was nearing obsession, and I couldn't figure out why.

The only possible explanation I could come up with was that she simply made me … happy. It had been so long since I felt true, unadulterated happiness. She provided that for me.

Speaking to her brought out something in me that I hadn't felt since I was a kid. Usually, I would spend my time with people who would temporarily fill the void of loneliness. With her, there was no loneliness, there was no avoiding negativity. I felt at peace.

I wanted more of that. I'd chase that feeling to the ends of the earth.

MCKENNA JAMES

Chapter 11

Maggie

I was a total idiot for agreeing to meet Edward after my shift finished.

I mean, really, what did I think I was doing? I had made such a thing out of the fact that I couldn't continue to spend time with Edward, that I would get too attached. Then he asked me to spend time with him, and I just agreed?

It was so stupid, but I didn't know how to resist him. That was part of the reason why I didn't want to see him at work in the first place.

Now, as I was about to finish my meeting with Abigail and Drew's teachers, my heart was pounding. I couldn't believe I was about to see him again. Would he want to have sex?

I assumed he would. Why else would he be asking me to meet him? I wasn't naïve. I didn't think that this meant he wanted to date me. I knew that he had no interest in dating anyone exclusively, and I didn't think I would be the exception to that rule.

Being that I wasn't the exception, I couldn't succumb to Edward again. No, I would meet with him because I had already agreed to, but I would only meet with him to inform him that we needed to cease any intimate relations. Yeah, that was good... I'd be entirely upfront that I wasn't interested in being a fling for him or anyone else. Hopefully he'd under-stand, and it wouldn't affect our relationship too much at work.

I left my meeting with the kids' teachers and entered the west wing of the palace. It was a quiet wing, mostly made up of guest bedrooms that were currently unused.

I heard footsteps coming from behind me and turned around to see Edward standing there, a smile on his face.

"Here, follow me," he said as he took my hands and pulled me into one of the guest bedrooms.

As soon as his hand touched mine, a familiar tingle of excitement ran down my spine. He shut the door behind us, and I had to pluck up the courage to tell him we couldn't do this anymore.

"Look, Edward, I'm not so sure this is a good idea."

"What?"

"You know, us seeing each other. It doesn't feel like the right thing to do. I mean, are you so sure this is a good idea?"

"No," he admitted. "To be honest, I'm not at all considering whether it's a good idea or not. I'm only considering one thing—the fact that I desperately need to have you."

He pulled me in close and kissed me once again. I told myself to pull away, but as his tongue explored mine, I couldn't bring myself to do it. It just felt so damned good.

Besides, if I was ending this now, what was one more kiss? I might as well enjoy his mouth one last time.

So, I did. For minutes. When he pulled away, he looked at me seriously.

"Do you really want to focus on how this isn't

a good idea? Or do you want to allow yourself to enjoy the moment? To enjoy me?"

I bit my lip. He had a point. Sure, I wasn't special enough to be hooking up with the Prince of England... This would never go anywhere, I'd never be his, and yeah... I may get a little attached.

Did I really want to let go of the fun that I was having now because of a potential attachment? No, I didn't think I did.

"If you want me to stop, I will. It's up to you."

"No," I said without thinking. "Don't stop."

He grinned and resumed kissing me.

I was a worried that someone could walk in on us. It wasn't the same as being in Edward's penthouse. At any moment, we could be barged in on.

It should have been enough to get me to stop, but oddly, it only encouraged me to continue. I thought about how taboo it would be for me to be caught in bed with Edward. Though I didn't want to be, the sneaking around made it all the sexier.

I did want this to be done fairly quickly, though. I wanted to get my fix and get out of here.

I also wanted him to dominate me the way he had before so to encourage that, I bit down on his lip to hint that I wanted this rough.

He got that hint.

He threw me down on the bed so roughly I bounced once. He started pulling his pants down, leaving his shirt on. In true quickie fashion, I did the same. Taking both my pants and panties off quickly.

He did lean down to give me oral again, like a true gentleman, but I didn't feel we had the time. Still, it was hard for me to resist, so I let him at least lick me a bit to prime my fervor.

I didn't know how he was so good at this, but he had easily given me the best oral I experienced in my life. He knew just how hard to press down on my clit. He ran his tongue in circles around me like no man had before. Last time we had sex; it took everything I had not to come from the oral alone.

I didn't want that. I was greedy. I wanted to feel his full, fat cock inside me, thrusting roughly. It had been so damn amazing the first time. I'd never slept with anyone who had a cock his size. It filled me completely and stimulated places I didn't even know existed before.

"Just jam it into me, we don't have much time," I said in a low voice, not wanting to be heard by anyone who might've been in the hall.

"Your wish is my command," he said softly as he pressed the tip of his cock against my pussy.

In one swift movement, he had jammed his stiff rod inside me. I was so soaking wet that it slid easily.

I threw my head back on the pillow and started moaning against my better judgement. It was like an involuntary action. He pushed against the walls of my pussy and exerted so much pleasure that I felt I had to verbalize it.

Thankfully, Edward had the quick thinking to cover my mouth with his hands so that my groans were muffled. This was even hotter. I loved when he exerted some control over my body.

I was so turned on right now.

I reminded myself that this would be my last time with him and encouraged myself to savor it.

He ran his hand up my shirt, groping at my

breasts as he moved in and out of me. He'd periodically pull his cock back, almost as if he was going to pull out of me, and then slammed his dick into me harshly. It felt like he was teasing me.

As much as I liked being teased, I feared we'd be interrupted and that this wouldn't last long. I wanted him to fuck me harder, but with his hand over my mouth, I couldn't very well say that.

So I grabbed his ass, digging my fingernails into his skin. Then I jerked him toward me.

He got the picture. He drilling me furiously, going from zero to one hundred in just a second, and I was trying to keep my moans to just that—moans.

I really wanted to scream.

He was hitting every pleasurable point inside my body. And it only became more intense when he reached down while he was furiously pumping me and started rubbing my clit to stimulate me.

It was too much to experience pleasure both on the inside and the outside. I couldn't take it. I thought he knew that. I had a feeling he wanted me to come before he did.

If that was his goal, he was about to succeed. I felt my vision go fuzzy and my mind go blank. It was like I wasn't human anymore. Instead, I was giving into some animalistic and primal part of my brain. The orgasm was rising within me, and I couldn't control it. I didn't want to control it. I wanted to succumb to him and his passion and desire for me.

So I did, and it rocked me to the core. I dug my hands into the sheets and grabbed handfuls of the blanket to keep from screaming. My legs began to shake wildly as my pussy pulsated on his cock. I could have sworn the orgasm went on for a full minute, but perhaps time just felt as though it had slowed down.

Within the time that I orgasmed, so had Edward. He made a quiet grunt as he pushed his cock to the hilt, deep within me. I felt his warmth spread out into me. I loved the way it felt. I loved the evidence that he had been inside me.

He pulled out of me and immediately got off the bed and grabbed his clothing.

Even though I wanted to end this, it oddly hurt

to see him get dressed so quickly. It was a reminder that this connection wasn't what I wanted it to be. For Edward, it was purely sexual, and when he got that sexual fix he was done. It wouldn't be like that for me. I needed more. I needed his attention, to be the only thought that crossed his mind. I urged to consume his heart and soul. I was head over heels, and I didn't know how I'd come to this point in such a short time.

I followed suit and started to dress as well.

"I really think you're the best sex I ever had," he said as he pulled his pants up.

This shocked me. I wasn't sure why. It probably shouldn't. He was just being nice after all. I was sure he probably said this to every woman he hooked up with.

Though if he did mean it... That would shock me. I knew he slept around. It didn't bother me much; he was the Prince of England and obviously he had messed around with hotter women than me. How could I possibly be the best with my minimal experience?

"Well, thank you, you're not too bad yourself," I teased.

"So, uh, listen… I'd love to see you again."

No! Okay, this was what I wanted to avoid. One last quickie was understandable. I couldn't let this continue the way it had. I had to be forthcoming with him. We couldn't continue to do this.

How should I word that in a way that wasn't mean? Damnit, I should have thought of this all earlier. I was never good on the spot.

"I don't know…" I muttered.

"What? Why? Didn't you have as good a time as I did?"

"Well, yes…"

"And is the sex as good to you?"

"Absolutely," I said eagerly, "you're positively amazing."

He grinned. "So, we're definitely doing this again then, right?"

Ugh, but no! We couldn't! The sex wasn't the problem. The problem was that I wanted more than this, and my emotions were already too deeply evolved. I had to back out of his situation to save myself from getting hurt. It was inevitable.

So why couldn't I say that? Why couldn't I tell him directly that this had to end promptly?

Because, despite my better judgement, I still had hope. I knew it was stupid. I knew there was no chance of Edward falling for me as I was falling for him. Yet, I held out hope anyway; and that stung.

I mean, even if Edward ever did like me, he couldn't do anything about it. He could never be serious with a woman like me. I wasn't fit for the royal family. I'd accepted that.

So I needed to stop fucking royal cock.

I willed myself to pluck up the courage and say this to him. Before I could open my mouth, he leaned in and kissed me. That shut me right the hell up.

"You're amazing Maggie, truly."

I bit my lip and allowed myself to be swept up by this compliment. In my mind, this compliment was about more than sex. Perhaps he had liked my personality. Perhaps he simply liked me.

I had to drill it into my head that all his compliments *were* about sex, though. He didn't really like me. He just liked fucking me.

"I … gotta go," I said as I grabbed my things and headed out of the room. I didn't even give him a chance to say goodbye. I just rushed out. I knew I wasn't going to end it right now, so the best thing I could do was get out of there before I became even more enthralled with the man.

Damn, I was a coward.

Chapter 12

Edward

I sat atop my horse as I waited for the match to start. I knew I should have been focusing on the game before me; polo was extremely dangerous after all, if you weren't focused, all I could think about was Maggie.

I looked out at the crowd. There were many royals who had come to watch the match. It was a beautiful day for polo. The sun was shining, the grass was lush, and people were prepared to be entertained. Yet, all I was fantasizing about was Maggie being here to watch me.

She wasn't, of course. She couldn't be. This was a prestigious event; it wasn't open to the public. It would be possible to invite her if I was dating her more seriously...

It was something I'd been considering a lot the

past few weeks, since my disastrous date with Angelique. Like Cecilia, she had attempted to sink her talons into me, luring me into a good time with the preface of just dinner—which led to dessert and her hoping we could be exclusive. I didn't do exclusivity. However, the more time I'd spent around Maggie, the longer we let our fling go on, the more entranced I was with the cute, little American; the more hesitant Maggie seemed to allow me into her life. I could understand why. She was worried we'd be caught in a compromising position. She was worried she'd look unprofessional. That wouldn't happen if I publicly claimed to be dating her.

That was a big step for me, though. Never had I committed to a woman like that. There was a lot of pressure on me, and it was genuinely understood that when I did commit to a woman, I had to be quite serious. She could become the princess after all.

Which was something that someone like Maggie very likely did not want to be. She had said many times over that she understood my desire to dismiss my royal responsibilities. I doubted she wanted any for herself.

Regardless, she wasn't even a proper Brit. She was American—though that was undisputedly what I loved about her even more so.

Either way, that was far too much to think about right now. She wasn't going to be officially dating me anytime soon. I wasn't ready for that commitment.

Still, I was enjoying my time with her thoroughly. Now when I thought about her, it simply wasn't about how I wanted to have her. It wasn't just desire. I thought about her as a person.

Like how much she had to struggle with the hospital bills for her father. That didn't seem even remotely fair to me, and I worried about it often. Why, during the hardest point in her life, should she be focused on finances? I mean, she had no idea the course her father's cancer would take, and yet she had to worry about money? It was barbaric.

Someone as kind as her didn't deserve it. She was such a sweet, nurturing soul. Most of the women I'd met were eager to go on vacation with me or head to the most exclusive clubs every weekend night. Maggie wasn't like that. She spent every moment she wasn't at work with her dad. She cleaned their flat, cooked for them, and made sure his every need was tended to. She not only worried about his physical health, she worried about him as a whole, making sure he never spent too much time alone and that he was in good spirits. She was an angel.

She deserved the world.

I'd ceased hanging out with any other women in recent weeks, my last date with Angelique was the breaking point. I knew it wasn't serious between me and Maggie yet, so it wasn't that I felt I had to be involved with anyone; it was just that no other women interested me in the slightest anymore. Spending time with any of them felt like a waste. The only person who actually made my time feel fulfilled was Maggie.

The match began suddenly, and I was pulled out of my reverie of Maggie and forced to play the game. I rose my mallet above my head as my horse charged toward the ball. The first hit was made by the opposing team, and I promptly raced my horse toward our goal to stop the ball in its tracks.

I was very good at polo, if I did say so myself. It was one of those things I just had a knack for. Ever since I was a young boy, I was interested in it, and as a member of the royal family, it was expected that I play.

I genuinely enjoyed it. Usually, polo was a release for me. It was an opportunity to escape my life and my feelings of loneliness and stress. It took all of my energy and focus, so everything else was left behind as I played.

That wasn't how I felt now. Normally, I was eager to use polo to avoid thoughts of my life. Right now, life wasn't so bad. It was actually very enjoyable. I couldn't have cared less about the game at hand.

So, I was understandably sloppy today. I hoped my teammates might carry me. Frankly, it felt so silly to me to care about the outcome of a game of polo when Maggie was worried about serious things like the outcome of her father's illness.

I did my best to keep up regardless. We almost got it through the opposing goal, but in the last moment, someone swooped in and hit the ball back. I eagerly rushed my horse over to go get it, being a little mindless about my surroundings.

I paid for it.

Suddenly, I felt a knock to my helmet, and then my world went black.

When I came to, I was no longer on my horse but instead on the ground. I was disoriented, unsure of what had happened, but people were now surrounding me.

"Wh-what?" I muttered.

"You got knocked off your horse!" I heard the familiar voice of Ms. Mitchell say to me.

Subsequently, I turned to see my mother kneeling in front of me.

"Edward? Are you alright?" she asked frantically.

"I … think so," I mumbled.

I wasn't sure how long I'd been out, but I didn't think it could've been more than a few seconds. My horse was still in front of me.

There was a ringing in my head, and I tried to sit up but was immediately dizzy. My mother promptly pushed me back down.

"No, no, stay there!" she said. "The ambulance has been called."

I groaned. "Mum, I don't need an ambulance."

"You absolutely do, and I won't hear more about it!" She turned to Ms. Mitchell. "Please make sure they can get in the gate."

"Right away," Ms. Mitchell said, sounding a little more panicked than I'd ever heard her be.

I really wasn't too worried about it, though. My head was definitely aching, and I didn't like the sense of vertigo I was experiencing. I was wearing a helmet. I didn't think it could be too bad.

As everyone shuffled around me, there was only one thought that kept consistently coming to my mind. I wasn't sure if it was the concussion that put the thought on repeat, or just my genuine concern, but regardless, I kept thinking the same thing over and over again…

MCKENNA JAMES

I had to help Maggie.

Chapter 13

Maggie

I was in the kitchen whipping up a lasagna that my father had requested for dinner, and against my better judgement, I obliged him. I knew he probably shouldn't have been eating something as heavy as lasagna, but it was rare these days that my father actually requested food of any kind, so I felt the need to get him what he wanted.

Apparently, lack of judgement was a common theme in my life lately.

Despite my determination to cut off Edward, I hadn't done so at all. We continued to secretly hook up, and I grew more and more attached to him every day.

That attachment had run out of control, really. I thought of Edward constantly. Even when I was working with the kids, I was always praying for Edward to pop up. He had become a constant fixture in my mind, and I was properly embarrassed about that fact. Still, I let it continue.

Simply because he was irresistible to me. Not to be crude, but I'd never had sex this good in my life. He sent my mind into places it'd never been before, and I couldn't give him up for the life of me. I wanted him every second of every day. It never ended.

I knew that was going to happen, though. I had nobody to blame but myself. I certainly didn't blame Edward, but I did want him badly.

It was pathetic, really. I mean, I was never going to be a serious girlfriend for him. He was a prince. He needed to date and subsequently marry someone who had similar social status. And that absolutely wasn't me and never would be. I wasn't the woman for him. No matter how much I wished I could be.

It wasn't just Edward's good looks that got me. After we would hook up, we'd hang out and talk about life, and he was just so easy to get on with. You'd think someone who had been told all his life how important he was would be a little egotistical, but he wasn't. He had a kind soul. He always listened about what was going on with my life. He made me feel cared for.

Which only made my feelings worse. If I wanted to stick to not having feelings for him, then I probably should have ceased talking to him after we had sex. I found rejecting his conversation was just as hard as rejecting his advances.

I was putting on a middle layer of lasagna and decided to load up a lot more eggplant and zucchini than I normally would. I may have been giving in to my dad's desires a bit, but I wouldn't tell him that this was a lasagna loaded with veggies and low-fat cheese. Hopefully he wouldn't even notice.

When I finished layering, I'd load it up with marinara and put noodles on top. It would take about an hour in the oven, but at least the house would smell amazing tonight. There were way too many nights lately where I succumbed to frozen meals because I was tired from work and from taking care of my dad. I really needed to cook more often.

I walked out of the kitchen to find my father in

the living room, watching some sitcom I didn't recognize.

"Is it cooking?" he asked eagerly.

"Sure is. Will be done in an hour. I'm glad you're so excited about this."

"Oh, I really am."

"So your appetite has been coming back?" I asked.

"Yes, day by day, it has." He smiled at me.

"Good. I'm glad to hear it." That had to be a good sign for his health.

"So, how's work been, my dear? I haven't gotten to talk to you too much lately with how tired I've been."

"It's honestly really, really great. I mean, I never imagined I'd one day work in a palace. Can't deny how cool it is."

"Yes, it really is," he agreed. "I've been emailing some friends and family back home and bragging about you." He grinned.

"Oh, Dad." I shook my head, though it was sweet how much pride he had in me.

174

"Allow me to brag about my daughter, please. You're the one great accomplishment in my life." He smiled at me. "So, how well do you know the royals? I mean, you know the kids, of course, but what about the queen?"

"I've met her," I said, nodding, "but I really don't know her too well. She seems nice, though. I do talk to the prince a lot more. He likes to hang out during some of the tutoring sessions because he likes to spend time with his younger siblings."

"Aw, well isn't that nice. It's just so neat that you actually get to spend time with the royal family."

It was, but lately I was wanting more.

I loved Edward, and I loved the kids, but I didn't want to have just a working relationship with them. I couldn't help but think about what it might be like to be more to them. If I was dating Edward, I'd be more than just their teacher—I'd be family.

How I longed to be that close to them all.

I couldn't keep fantasizing about it. Where was daydreaming going to get me? That was only going to make me more attached to the idea of a life that I was never going to have.

"Well, I'm proud of you, honey. I really am."

"Thanks, Dad."

If nothing else, I was proud of me for getting this job as well, even if I did have Edward to thank for it. It did allow me to keep up on hospital payments … barely. I still had a long way to go for the medical bills to be paid off, and I had to make the smallest payments that I could. Still, it allowed me to get out from under the stress a bit.

I leaned back on the couch as I watched TV with my dad. My phone buzzed in my pocket, and I pulled it out to find a breaking news alert.

"Breaking News: Prince Edward injured in a polo accident."

I shot up on the couch, fully alert as I waited for the article to load. My father noticed something was wrong immediately.

"What? What is it?" he asked.

"It's the prince. Apparently, he was injured in a polo game," I answered, my heart pounding as I willed my damn phone to load faster!

When it did, I speed-read through the article. Apparently, he had been hit in the head with another player's mallet. He had fallen off his horse and was knocked unconscious.

"Oh my God," I muttered.

"What?" my father asked again.

"He was knocked unconscious. I have to call Ms. Mitchell and make sure he's alright," I said before I walked outside.

I felt sick to my stomach thinking about Edward being injured. What if it was serious? I had the strong urge to go to him, wherever he was, but I knew that would be wholly inappropriate. Why should I be allowed at whatever hospital he was at? I was nothing to him.

But he was everything to me.

"Hello?" Ms. Mitchell answered the phone.

"Ms. Mitchell, hi. I just heard about Prince Edward. Is he alright?"

"Yes, yes, he's going to be. Apparently, he has a minor concussion and will need to rest a lot this week, but he should make a full recovery with no lasting damage."

I let out a large sigh of relief. "Good, good. I'm so glad to hear that," I said.

"Very sweet of you to check up on him, my dear."

Right … yeah. As an employee, my gesture is only sweet. God, I hated that I felt so close to him but to everyone else I was so distant. Not that I wanted people to know about us or anything. It was frustrating to have someone mean so much while I felt I meant so little.

"We'll be seeing you tomorrow afternoon at the palace?"

"Yes, of course," I told her.

"Fantastic. Goodnight now, dear." She hung up.

Even though I knew Edward was fine, I felt desperate to know more. Where was he staying? Could I visit? Did he need anything? Who was taking care of him?

These were all silly questions, of course, because he was the Prince of England. I didn't think he needed me to worry about who was fussing after him. The whole palace would be fussing after him.

I wanted it to be m who was by his side. I wanted to be the one caring for him, getting him back to full health. Dammit, why couldn't it be me?

I had to take a deep breath before I went back in to see my father. It was stupid how much I had to calm myself down. Edward would be fine. He didn't need me. I needed to be reasonable about this whole thing.

I couldn't be reasonable. Which was why I had never intended to get this involved with him in the first place!

I knew that I had to end things. If I didn't, how hurt was I going to be if I let this go on for months? I'd be unavoidably attached to Edward. And, subsequently, he wouldn't be attached to me.

So. what would happen when he met someone? As in, met someone for real? A woman he could actually take with him to the throne?

It would absolutely break my heart. I wasn't sure how I'd recover from that. Which meant I needed to end things before I watched him ride off into the sunset with another woman.

I couldn't tell him right now, of course, since he was recovering from a concussion. That would just be cruel and unnecessary. I'd wait until he healed up.

I wanted to at least text him to ask how he was doing, make sure he was alright. I feared if he was in the hospital that his cell phone was in somebody else's hands, so asking how he was doing might give me away. I couldn't have that.

I desperately feared anybody finding out what Edward and I had been up to. It would make me look awful, and potentially; it could even put me in the spotlight. Well, I had zero desire to be in the spotlight. I wouldn't feel good being written about in the tabloids as the American tramp sleeping with the prince. So it was best that our relationship stayed secret from everyone. So far, we'd done a good job of hiding it.

I finally readied myself to go inside and shut the door quietly behind me. I was hoping my father wouldn't hear me come in and thus wouldn't ask me how Edward was. He did hear, and of course he asked.

"How is the prince?"

"He's fine," I answered. "A small concussion, but he'll be alright."

"Good, good. I could see you were very worried about him."

I could tell he was prying a bit.

"Yes, well, Edward is a very good man. He has always been extremely kind to me. It would be awful if anything was seriously wrong with him."

"Right." He nodded but was still a bit suspicious.

That night, as we ate lasagna on the couch, it was all I could do to focus on the TV and the conversation with my father. In the back of my mind, it was only Edward I wanted to speak to. I was eager to go into work the next day, hoping that he'd find his way into my lesson, and I could make sure that he was okay.

Unfortunately, that wasn't exactly how the day

went.

An hour into my tutoring sessions with Drew and Abigail, Edward still hadn't shown up. It was starting to worry me. Was he not yet back on his feet?

I tried to focus on the lessons we had today and not preoccupy myself with Edward's health, but that didn't go so well. The longer I put off asking about Edward, the more anxious I became. Eventually, I just blurted it out to Drew and Abigail.

"So, how is your brother doing? I heard about his accident." I tried to sound casual but it came off as anything but.

"Ooh, do you want to know how Edward is because you like him?" Abigail chimed teasingly.

I could feel my cheeks go rosy red. "I like him as a friend, of course."

"I think you like-like him," Abigail continued to tease.

Was it that obvious?

Drew didn't tease me at all, though, thankfully.

"He is doing okay. He has a headache, but he'll live. Mum is making sure he has nurses with him all

182

the time."

"Is it still that serious?" I asked, growing worried.

"I don't think so. I think my mum is just over-reacting. I saw him this afternoon, and he seemed fine. Maybe a little tired."

"Yeah, and he can't watch any movies! He's super bored!" Abigail said.

I had heard that, actually. That you couldn't watch TV or read after a concussion. Something about needing to allow the brain to heal, though admittedly I didn't entirely understand it.

"We're going to go visit him after our lesson, so he'll be less bored. Want to come?" Abigail asked.

"Oh, no, no. I'd better not. He should get his rest, be only with his family."

I was relieved to know he was being well cared for.

That week dragged on slowly. Every day, I was hoping Edward would be well enough to walk around the palace and intrude on a lesson. Every day, I was sorely disappointed. After my ribbing from Abigail,

I stopped asking about him. I didn't want anything to seem suspicious to the kids.

At the end of the week, I went home and grabbed our mail to find I had another letter from the hospital. It sent a wave of panic through me. Even though I'd been making the minimum payments on my bill, if they were sending a letter to ask for another payment this month, I wouldn't have the money. Or if my minimum payment amount for each month went up, I couldn't afford that either.

I walked into my flat and sat at the kitchen table before I opened it, fully prepared to have a meltdown if this letter changed my financial burden in any way. I had finally felt like I'd gotten ahold of my finances, and now I was about to get pushed behind again? Just my damned luck.

I couldn't see any reason for the hospital to send a letter except for a bill. So, I braced myself and tore the envelope open.

I was shocked at what I saw.

It was an invoice for a payment … except I hadn't made a payment.

The hospital seemed to think that I did. For the life of me, I didn't know why.

It showed the balance for my father's bills at zero. Everything was paid off. The balance was taken care of.

That wasn't possible.

I tried not to allow myself to be relieved because, clearly, this was a massive mistake. Obviously, someone else had made a payment, and it had been credited to me. I couldn't see any other reason for this to happen.

I definitely had to call them tomorrow and sort this all out. Hey, at least I wasn't getting an additional bill in the mail.

MCKENNA JAMES

Chapter 14

Edward

This was truly the most boring week of my entire damned life.

The whole week, my mother had me on round-the-clock care. It seemed wholly unnecessary to me, but she had a nurse checking my vitals multiple times a day. They brought me soups and electrolyte drinks to make sure I stayed hydrated. They made sure the lights in the room stayed dim and that I wasn't playing on my phone or anything.

Not that I would. The doctor had made it abundantly clear that for my head to heal properly, I needed to stay away from reading or watching anything.

Which was unfortunate because, frankly, I really, really wanted to text Maggie. I wanted to ask if she'd visit me. Man, this would be a lot less boring if she was here.

Though I did have people from the palace stop in a lot. My siblings also kept me company whenever they were available, and my mother was checking in on me all the time. Still, when they left and I had nobody to talk to, I was horribly bored.

I tried to sleep, but there was only so much of that I could do until I was entirely awake.

I decided to give my lawyer a call. I could do that without looking at my phone, I just had to use voice commands.

I'd called him the night of my concussion and instructed him to find out what hospital Maggie's father had been treated at and subsequently pay off all his hospital bills. I wanted to see how things were going with that.

"Hello, offices of Davis and Smith," the receptionist answered.

"Hello, it's Prince Edward Wellington. I just wanted to check in with Mr. Smith on the matter we discussed earlier this week."

"Yes, sir, Prince Edward. One moment

please." An old classical tune filled the brief air before my lawyer's greeting.

"Oh, Prince Edward, I was just about to call you. Everything has been handled with Miss Spencer's father's medical bills. The balance with the hospital has been paid in full."

"Fantastic! I'm so happy to hear that." I smiled to myself. This was going to make things so much easier on Maggie.

"No problem at all. Is there anything else I can get done for you?"

"Nope, that will be all for now. Thank you again."

"Of course, Prince Edward. I am wishing you a speedy recovery."

At least that was one positive thing that came from this accident. Although I did get a concussion, it was purely a selfless act for obsessively considering Maggie's hardships and consequently deciding to assist.

I should have thought about it more before making the final decision. I really wasn't sure why I didn't. Impulse, perhaps. Instinct. I supposed sometimes it took a mallet to the head to force me to come to my senses.

Though I'd be happy to avoid all future mallets if at all possible.

All week, I'd been avoiding calling Maggie. Though I'd texted her many times before, I'd never actually phoned her. For some reason, that felt a lot more intrusive. I'd suppose it was because people rarely just called anyone anymore. I didn't want to seem too attached.

The thing was, I couldn't help being attached. All I could think about right now was how badly I wanted to speak with her. I wondered if she wanted to speak to me too.

So, I commanded my phone to call her. She answered on the third ring; I'd counted.

"Hello?" Her sweet voice sent a shiver down my spine. I hadn't realized how much I'd missed it this week until right now.

"Maggie, hey. It's Edward."

She chuckled a little. "Yes, Edward, I do have

caller ID. How are you? I heard about the accident, and I've been worried sick."

So, she'd been worried about me, huh? That seemed like a pretty good sign to me.

"I'm doing okay. Though I am horribly bored. Do you think you could come visit? I'm at the palace, I'm not sure if you know that."

"I do," she said. "I heard from the kids. But, uh, I'm not sure I should."

"Oh, come on, Maggie. I'm injured. If you don't come to me, it'll force me to come to you. If I do that, I might accidentally injure myself again. If you're the reason the heir to the throne is hurt, all of England will hate you," I teased.

"All of England hating me is actually one of the reasons I don't think I should come," she answered seriously.

"What? Why is that?"

"Because... Edward, how would it look if I came to visit you? People ... they talk. If anyone saw me..."

"Maggie, we're in the palace. I just have nurses

checking in on me. I'm all by myself, and we're safe within these palace walls. Please, just come visit. I promise you; word won't get out."

She sighed. "Okay, fine. Because you're not feeling well. That's the only reason. I'll come by when I'm done with my shift."

"Perfect, I'll see you then."

I hung up the phone with a grin on my face. I couldn't have been more eager to see her. Suddenly, I felt a lot less bored. At least now I got to fantasize about the fact that I'd be with Maggie in only a few hours.

Normally that thought would get me a bit revved up, but I was in no state to accept any sexual desire. My body shut that all down immediately. I had a headache just rolling over in bed. I certainly didn't want to do anything as strenuous as having sex.

The minutes passed slowly as I waited for her. I kept glancing at the grandfather clock that was on the other side of my dimly-lit room. I didn't know if I was supposed to be reading clocks, but I didn't much care at the moment.

When I finally heard a knock at my door, my heart began to race.

"Come in," I said softly, as I prayed it wasn't just another nurse.

It wasn't. Maggie walked in slowly, hesitantly, looking around the room as if there would be someone else here.

"It's just me, I promise you," I assured her. "Come on, come in. Keep me company. I'm bored out of my mind."

She looked hesitant but pulled up a chair. She didn't get too close to my bed, though. She was feet away from me.

"Hey, I don't bite."

"Yeah, well, this looks a lot less suspicious," she said.

"Suspicious to who? Maggie, you worry too much. It's just us here. Relax a little."

"I can't relax… It's my job on the line, Edward, and you know I really need this job."

I sighed. "Alright, as long as you're hanging

out, I guess that's all I can ask for."

"So, how are you doing? I've been thinking about you."

"I'm okay. I think I'm more bothered with my mum and everyone in the palace fussing over me than I am my actual head pain. It's getting annoying, fending off everyone."

"They're just concerned about you. I would be too."

I smiled at her. "Well, I wish it was you fussing over me instead."

"Me too," she said, a little sadly.

I wasn't expecting that reaction.

"What? What is it?" I asked.

"No, nothing." She shrugged it off.

"Seriously, what is it?" I pressed.

She didn't have an opportunity to answer. In walked one of my nurses with a tray of food.

"I've got to check on your vitals, Edward," she said to me.

"Right, of course."

She began to take my blood pressure as well as

my heart rate, and I could see that Maggie was incredibly uncomfortable. I felt a little bad. I'd insisted she wouldn't be seen, and then somebody walked in.

She really was overreacting a bit. We weren't doing anything uncouth. She was sitting halfway across the room, for crying out loud! This woman was a professional. What was she going to do? Run down the hall and tell everyone who would listen that the royal tutor was in my room? We were friends! It was no big deal.

Still. I felt for her discomfort and didn't want her to experience any more of it.

"You know, I don't think I need to be checked on again tonight," I told the nurse.

She side-eyed me a bit. "I can't let you go unchecked all night." Then she glanced over at Maggie and seemed to understand why I wanted to be alone. "Perhaps I can push off your next check until midnight."

"That would be awesome." I smiled at her. "Thank you."

She nodded and then left the room.

As soon as the door shut behind her, Maggie stood.

"I should go."

"Maggie, wait, please," I said, sounding more desperate than I'd intended.

"Edward, I shouldn't be here. Really. Anyone could come in at any time and—"

"She was the only one who would ever come in unannounced, and she just said she'd leave us alone until midnight. What's the harm? I mean, we're both adults. Even if people did assume, we were dating, would that be so wrong?"

"No," she said definitively. "Their assumption that we were dating wouldn't be so bad. The thing is they'd never assume that. Because you're a prince and I'm a tutor. So, what they're going to think we're doing is hooking up. I don't want to be known as the royal whore."

"Well, you're not a royal, so technically..." I gave her a playful smile.

She was unamused by my joke. "Edward, I'm going to go."

"Maggie, please. Nobody would think that of you. You're a sweet, charming, honorable woman. You're here to keep a friend company while he has a concussion because he's begging you to. It's nothing more than that."

She sighed as she sat back down. "Fine, I can stay a little longer."

"Thank you." I smiled. "But, uh, do you think you could stay a bit closer to me?"

She laughed. "What? You want me to inch my chair closer?"

"Even closer than that." I patted the bed next to where I was lying.

"Edward, tell me you did not call me in here for a booty call!" She stood up angrily. "I absolutely would never have intercourse with you when you're in this state."

I had to laugh at her use of the word intercourse. She was so funny. I loved the way she spoke. It wasn't like anyone I'd ever met.

"I don't want to have sex, Maggie. Are you kidding? I'm injured. I have no sexual drive right now. I just want to be near you."

She looked skeptical. "Really? Why?"

"Why do you think? Because you comfort me. Because I love your presence. Just come cuddle me for a bit, please."

I could see it in her eyes. She wanted to say no, but she couldn't resist this request. Why should she? It was a pretty simple request.

She walked over to me slowly, slid her shoes off, and then climbed up next to me on the bed. We'd done this before, but only after sex. It was never like this—never clothed and never innocent.

When she crawled up under my arm, it immediately felt different. It was somehow more intimate. I wouldn't think that lying with somebody fully clothed would feel more intimate than undressed. Somehow, it just did. It was nice.

I could smell her hair, and I leaned into it, putting my cheek on the top of her head.

"Thank you," I whispered.

"For what?" she asked.

"For staying … I really missed you."

I could feel her body tense up as I said that, and I wondered if I'd said something wrong. A moment later, she responded.

"I missed you too."

"So, what do you want to do until midnight?" I asked her. "I wish we could watch movies or something, but unfortunately I'm not allowed to do that while I'm healing."

She looked up at me. "I guess we could just talk?"

"Yeah." I smiled down at her. "Let's do that. Let's just talk. How are things with your dad?" I wondered if she knew about the hospital bill yet.

"They're good … a little stressful. I mean, he does seem to be doing better this week. It doesn't matter how well he seems to do, I'm constantly worried that I'm going to lose him. I mean, to be honest, I used to be afraid of losing him even when he was healthy, but I guess his cancer really amplified those fears."

"Really?" This confused me. "Why would you ever worry about him while he was healthy?"

"Oh, well, I guess that was just a consequence of losing my mom." She had never told me about her mother, not outside of passing moments. Though because of how she went unmentioned, I had understood she wasn't in the picture and never dared to ask more. "I think when you lose a parent, it really puts mortality into perspective. When I lost my mom… I just couldn't imagine having to go through that pain and grief ever again. So I feared that happening with my dad a lot."

Somehow, I knew exactly what she meant. "That went through my head a lot after my father passed," I told her.

"It did?"

"Yeah. I really began to care so much more for my mum. I mean, I have always loved my mum, of course. It's different after a parent dies, you know? My mum became everything I had after my dad passed."

"No, I totally get it. I feel the same way. My dad is everything to me. I don't even mind taking care of him, juggling hospital bills, spending all my

200

nights in. It gets lonely sometimes, I guess, when my dad is too tired to talk to me."

"It does, huh? Maybe I should keep you company? Come visit with your dad?" I suggested.

"Oh my God, that would be so cool! He would flip out if he got to meet the Prince of England! That would be so nice of you."

That wasn't how I meant it.

I was trying to gauge her reaction to me meeting her father, not suggest that I'd visit him for fun as a kind gesture. I didn't want to get to know her dad as a kind gesture...

I wanted to get to know her dad as her boyfriend.

I didn't say this out loud. It felt really weird to say. What if she took it badly?

I normally didn't fear rejection. One, because I rarely ever was rejected, and two, because I didn't care enough about the women I asked out to be bothered by it.

I cared about Maggie. Man, did I care about her. More than I'd ever cared for a woman in my life.

So, to be rejected by her … that would hurt. It would hurt more than my throbbing head right now.

If she was going to reject my advances, I wanted to savor this. I didn't want it to happen when I was already stressed and in pain. I'd rather I found out later, when I was healed.

Though I hoped I wouldn't have to be rejected at all.

"Anyway, I don't want to talk too much about myself. What about you? How are things going in your life?" she asked.

"Oh, well, uh … they're going." I forced a smile. "Actually, I've enjoyed my life a lot recently. I definitely enjoy hearing about you, especially when hearing about your family history."

"Really? Why's that?"

"I guess because it's so unknown to me. I mean, you pretty much get to know mine. My entire ancestry is out there for the world to see. But you … you're a secret. Your life is hidden from the world, which seems nice."

"Not to brag, but it is kind of nice," she agreed.

"I really don't know how you do it, dealing with people always prying into your life. I mean, you got hit on the head with a mallet, and I got a damn alert on my cell phone!"

"You bloody well did not!" I groaned. "Lord, the things they turn into breaking news…"

"Well, it was breaking news to me at least."

My heart fluttered when she said that. It gave me hope that whatever we had between us was as serious to her as it was to me. I desperately wanted that to be the case.

"It's really nice to be able to talk to someone about how I felt after my dad died, though," I told her. "I haven't really gotten to do that with anyone."

"Really? I would've thought everyone would've asked you about it, would have wanted to hear you discuss it."

"Sure, yeah, they might want to hear it, but that didn't mean I wanted to share it. Most people, when they ask about my father, are looking for some gossipy details about his passing. As I'm sure you know, it was a car accident. He happened to be driving himself, which was a rarity, and everyone wanted to speculate whether he was drunk or on some kind of drugs, even though it was reported he wasn't. I mean, people think the royal family has some kind of pull with the media where we can get them to not publish our dirty little secrets, but in my experience, it's the opposite that's true. We can't get them to stop."

"My God, that's so awful," she said. I could hear it in her voice, she truly thought so. "Nobody deserves to go through that after they have a parent pass away. I wish people had the good sense to leave you and your family alone. You guys do not deserve to be continually bothered this way."

"You're sweet." I kissed the top of her head. "I think that's one of the reasons I shirk away so much of my responsibilities, though."

She wasn't following. "How do you mean?"

"Well, after my father passed, everyone would talk about how I'd come into the throne. The weight of the amazing king my father was just came raining down on me. I couldn't take it. I loved my mother so dearly, but at every opportunity I felt like I was such a disappointment to her. I didn't want to be, so I avoided talking to her about anything I needed to do. I avoided thinking about it. I even avoided being home much of the time."

"You seem to be at the palace a lot now," she observed.

"Yes, well, frankly, I think you have something to do with that. You and my siblings, of course. I have always made time for them. Even with them, I feel like I'm failing. I could be a better big brother to them."

"Are you kidding me? Edward, you have no idea how those kids really see you."

"What?" I asked.

"They worship the ground you walk on. Those children adore you. You are the perfect role model to them; I can promise you that. If anything, you're too good of a role model for them."

I was honored to hear this from her. "How could I be too good of a role model?"

"By being a lot to live up to. Sometimes Drew

gets really down on himself when he can't do something as well as you can, like riding horses."

"He does?" I didn't like hearing that part, though. "He really shouldn't. That boy is a much better kid than I was at his age. He's smart, responsible, he's probably the one who actually should end up king instead of me."

"Aw, don't say that," she said gently. "You're going to be an amazing king, Edward. You are kind, considerate, and you seem pretty responsible to me. For a guy with a reputation as a partier, I don't see you partying much."

That was only because I'd stopped since meeting her. I didn't feel the need to go out anymore. If I had a free moment, I'd rather it be spent with Maggie.

Frankly, if we ended up together, I could confidently say I didn't think I'd ever party again. I felt no need. Going out and meeting women was filling a void for me that I didn't need filled with Maggie by my side.

"I hope that's true," I said.

"Just marry someone who would make a good

206

queen. Someone who will really guide you in becoming a good king, you know?"

Yeah, I thought I did know.

I wasn't sure how long we kept talking, nor did I really know when the conversation stopped. At some point, I drifted off to sleep with her still in my arms.

When I was awoken by light streaming in from the doorway, I yawned and looked over at where I thought Maggie would still be.

To my dismay, she was gone. It was my nurse coming in. She must have left before midnight, but did she say goodbye? I couldn't remember.

"How are you feeling, Edward?" the nurse asked me.

"Not so well," I said, now that I knew she had left.

I couldn't blame her for leaving. I knew she didn't want to be caught in my bed, and she knew the nurse was coming in at midnight. I just wished I was able to text her.

I hoped she'd drop by again tomorrow.

MCKENNA JAMES

Chapter 15

Maggie

"What? No, that can't be possible," I said into the phone. "Can you check again? I know it must be a mistake."

"I am very positive this is no mistake. Honestly, we've never had a mistaken payment. Your bill was most definitely paid off by an anonymous donor."

"That can … happen?" I asked. "You have no idea who it was?"

"We are not at liberty to disclose. Your balance is definitely paid off, and you do not owe the hospital."

"Oh … okay," I said, shocked. "Thank you then."

"You're very welcome. Have an excellent day."

I hung up the phone, still a little confused.

I had been so sure that it was a mistake that they thought my father's bill was paid off. It didn't seem possible. It was thousands of dollars. Who could possibly pay that off?

Then it hit me. Of course I knew who paid it off. I should have known earlier…

It was Edward.

I wasn't sure why he wasn't my first thought. I guessed I simply didn't consider he would go behind my back to do this.

It infuriated me.

Perhaps I should have been grateful. I mean, I was most definitely relieved that I no longer had these bills to pay, that was true. Outside of that, I was angry.

I didn't want to be his charity case. This oddly made me feel like some kind of prostitute.

Okay, perhaps that was dramatic. Edward definitely wasn't paying me for sex. This did feel like some weird kind of quid pro quo thing. I didn't like it.

It would be one thing if we were dating. If this

was serious, then I could understand him taking a vested interest and getting involved with my finances.

We weren't serious! He'd always been super clear about the fact that he didn't want to be. So, it made no sense why he would pop up and pay this off for me.

I absolutely did not like it or feel good about it in the slightest. As stressed as I was, that was my financial burden. I didn't want it on Edward.

Though it wasn't really a burden for him, was it? That was something else that made me so angry. The problem that had become the greatest stressor of my life was nothing to him. He could pay it and not bat an eye. Which only made me more of his pity case.

I was fuming as I stepped inside the palace and into the dining quarters. I had called the hospital on my dinner break because I didn't know when else to call. I couldn't do it while I was at home. I didn't want to alert my father to the mix-up. I tried to keep billing information away from him as much as possible. I didn't think it was something he should be thinking about.

"What's wrong?" Millie immediately asked me as soon as I sat.

I'd really come to enjoy Millie's company since I started working here. I'd come to know a lot about her life, just as she knew a lot about mine.

She didn't know about Edward. I'd kept that a secret from almost everyone. Not that I thought Millie would rat me out or anything. I really didn't, but I didn't want anyone to see me as Edward's booty call. I was afraid it might spark rumors about why I got this job in the first place.

"Oh, it's nothing." I tried to brush it off.

"It doesn't look like nothing. Spill the tea, girl," she pressed before sipping her water, the slang expression for 'gimme the gossip.'

I groaned. "It's just... I just found out that my dad's hospital bills were paid off."

She chuckled awkwardly. "Okay ... guess I'm not exactly understanding the problem. That's a good thing, right?"

"Yes, or it would be if I was the one to pay them off, but I didn't."

"So. who did?" she asked.

"I don't know for sure, but I expect it was the prince."

It felt weird to call him that as I never referred to him in a formal manner. To me, he was just Edward. If I called him that to Millie, she would know that we were closer than I let on.

I didn't see a reason not to tell her he was the one who paid, though. Surely, I could do that without disclosing our entire relationship.

"Aw, well that's really sweet of him! He must have heard through the grapevine about your dad and took steps to help him. That's really nice. I don't see why you're upset."

"I mean, yes, it's really nice, but … I don't know. I can't help but feel like he's trying to manipulate me."

"Manipulate you? Into doing what exactly?" Millie stared on.

"Just…" How could I explain this without revealing too much? "He's been a bit flirtatious, and it just feels like … I don't know." I was stumbling on my words.

Suddenly she smiled and nodded. "Ah, yes, I understand."

"What?" I asked.

"You and the prince. You've got a little thing going on."

"Uh, no, I didn't mean to say—"

"Now you're worried that, what? He wants something in return for doing you such a grand gesture?"

"Millie, can I confide in you?" She nodded eagerly, scooting closer as if she knew the details were juicy. "You promise it will never go any further?"

"Yes, Maggie!! We're friends, love. Just spill the tea already before it gets cold!"

I inhaled a quaking breath and spit it out in one strung together sentence, as if I said it any slower, I'd lose my confidence. "We've been sneaking around and seeing each other. Not as often as I like. But we've... Well, we've been rather promiscuous, and I think I'm falling for him, but in my mind, I know we could never be, you know? I'm so confused, Millie. I don't know what to do!"

My fears were out there now, everything I'd been struggling to tell Edward was now confided in Millie. I could only pray she'd keep her word and hold my secrets.

I couldn't continue speaking to her about this. I didn't want her to know all the sordid details. I didn't want anyone to know.

I may have just blown that, all because I was angry about Edward paying for my dad's hospital bills.

"Oh, crap. I, uh ... gotta get back to work," I lied, and pretending to check the time on my watch.

"Okay, sure. I'm here if you ever need to talk," she said. "Don't worry, your secret is safe with me."

I was worried. Extremely worried.

I stood and walked away. I was still angry, but now I was also entirely stressed that I'd just shared my biggest secret.

I had to trust that Millie wouldn't say anything, though. That was all I could do now.

I was furious with myself for making such a big mistake.

I was furious with Edward too! He shouldn't have done this. If he wanted to help me, why didn't he come forward and ask me? Why did he have to do it anonymously? I mean, surely he knew it wouldn't be truly anonymous. He knew I'd find out.

I couldn't say for sure that it meant he wanted something from me. I mean, he was already getting laid, what more could he want? I did think it suggested a weird dynamic. "Hey, thanks for having sex with me, here's all your debt paid off." I hated the way it made me feel.

I had to confront him, but how and when?

I couldn't do it now. I mean, I could… I could call or text him, but he wasn't in town. I didn't think this was the kind of conversation I wanted to have over the phone.

A few days after he recovered, he went on a trip. Evidently, the queen tried to talk him out of it,

216

but he insisted he was healed and could go. It was some kind of diplomatic endeavor that had been planned for six months, and he didn't want to let anyone down.

We'd been keeping in loose contact through his recovery. After our night of cuddling, I ran off completely stressed. Not that I didn't love the time I'd spent with him, I absolutely did. That was exactly part of the reason why I ran off.

I couldn't handle being that close to him, speaking to him so intimately. It felt so good to be in his arms. As he fell asleep on me, I kept thinking about how we could do this every night. If we lived together, we could stay up late talking and fall asleep in each other's arms. I even considered how nice it would be to wake up to him every day...

It was silly, a ridiculous fantasy, and I couldn't continue to indulge it. I was never going to be that woman for him, and yet I laid in his arms as if I possibly could be. I was ashamed of my lack of willpower and embarrassed by how deeply I liked him.

He did seem to like me too, but I was smart

enough to know that it wasn't going to spill over into relationship territory. He liked me like a best friend he could occasionally have sex with. He didn't like me as a serious, intimate girlfriend.

I had considered ending it after that night, but I was waiting for him to heal. Then shortly after he did, he told me he was leaving the country. So my plan was to explain things when he got back.

I was going to be honest and forthcoming. I was going to say that I cared deeply for him, but I knew we could never be. I was going to ask him to please not reach out to me any further because I couldn't resist him, and I didn't want to continually be sucked back into his life. I was going to politely tell him that this was over and ask that he respect my wishes.

Now? Screw being polite. I was going to give him a piece of my mind. He'd hear about how inappropriate it was for him to do such a thing ... how he should have asked me. If he was doing a genuinely kind, honest gesture, he would have asked!

I'd wait until he came back, though. When I

gave him a piece of my mind, I really wanted it to be in person.

I felt my phone buzz in my pocket. I pulled it out to find it was Edward... Maybe his ears were burning.

>>This is nightmarishly boring. Wishing I was back in London with you.

I couldn't help but roll my eyes. I was tired of his sweet talk. Now that he'd paid the hospital bill behind my back, I felt that all his chatter was just a way to manipulate me into doing what he'd wanted. I wasn't going to fall for it any longer.

>>We need to talk.

My reply seemed to worry him.

>>What? What about?

>> We'll talk when you get back. What day will you arrive?

>> Friday. Is something wrong? Can you at least tell me what this is about?

>>Meet me after my shift Friday?

>>Yes, of course.

I didn't explain any further than that. How

could I? If I'd told him anything more serious he would've asked me a million questions.

It would just have to wait until we saw each other once again.

Chapter 16

Edward

I'd been stressed out ever since I got Maggie's text saying that we needed to talk. She wouldn't explain why. I'd called many times, but she never picked up.

I could definitely sense she was mad, but I had no clue why. Because of that, I was desperate to get home.

Or, rather, I should say I was more desperate to get back home than usual. Because I always wanted to leave these diplomatic tours. They were exhausting.

I shouldn't complain, I knew that. Some people were working sixty-hour weeks in factories just to make ends meet for their families. I went on cushy press tours. I wasn't unaware of how privileged I was.

Still, I didn't think the general public understood that it was actual work. I'd met so many people in the past week. I had to shake so many hands, take so many photos. My feet were aching by the end of every day. All the while, I had to worry about what stresses were waiting for me back home.

At least today would be the day I flew home. I took solace in that. I was still obsessively checking my phone to see if Maggie had contacted me at all. She hadn't.

A lot of other people had.

It was weird… I normally had a few messages from royal officials, but suddenly I had ten friends texting me at the same time. Every text was all the same thing—a link to an article.

My heart sank. This couldn't be good.

I braced myself before I clicked it, and it was worse than I thought.

"Prince Edward Caught Taking Advantage of the Royal Nanny," the headline read.

This was so not good.

I skimmed the article quickly at first, but sure

enough, they named Maggie specifically. Though they stupidly called her the nanny instead of what she really was—my siblings' tutor.

I wasn't sure where they got their information from, and for a moment, I had no time to think about it. I only had one concern—this was going to severely hurt Maggie.

I wondered if this was what she wanted to speak with me about. Then I looked at the article again and realized it was from today. No, that couldn't be it then.

Which was awful because if she had something to talk to me about before, this wasn't going to help matters.

I tried to call Maggie right away … no answer, as usual.

I put the phone down and tried to breathe through it as I read the article more seriously. I didn't want to. I wanted to turn off my phone and pretend this wasn't happening. I had to know what exactly these people knew. Perhaps it wasn't much? Perhaps it didn't provide a lot of proof.

I was very, very wrong.

Not only did they have details about us flirting around the palace, they had actual pictures! There was a blurry photo of us in the garden—Maggie all wet, me peeling my shirt off.

This certainly looked bad.

There was another photo of us at the museum kissing. Well, I definitely couldn't deny that.

It all looked awful. At the end of the article, some anonymous source had been quoted saying that I had the nanny in my room until midnight while I was recovering. "Frankly, I find it all egregious that he cannot even keep it in his pants when ill."

We didn't even do anything!

I immediately felt guilty. Maggie had been so damn worried about that night, and what had I done? I assured her over and over again that it was no big deal, that nobody would notice us, that nobody would care…

Nothing could've been further from the damn truth.

I was the one who pushed her into this. It was

all my fault. If she was livid with me, she definitely had a right to be.

The worst part of this whole article, though, wasn't the pictures or the details of when we spent time together. It was the fact that they made me seem like a predator. It was as if I preyed on the nanny, pressured her into doing things with me.

That wasn't true. Maggie liked me. If they knew Maggie, they'd know she couldn't be pressured into doing anything she didn't want to. She rejected me at one point.

Why did they immediately leap to me being a predator? I mean, I supposed it was because she worked under me, but that didn't mean we couldn't have a consensual relationship.

I felt sick to my stomach. At first, I only felt bad for Maggie, but I was starting to get worried for myself. If this spun out of control, I could get a reputation as a predator.

My phone started buzzing, and I grabbed it quickly, praying that it would be Maggie. It wasn't.

It was my mum.

I immediately cringed. I didn't want to talk to her. I didn't want to tell her about the mistakes I'd made. She was going to be so upset with me, especially the way this article was written. It made me look like a monster.

I considered ignoring the call, allowing it to go to voicemail. I couldn't bring myself to do it. I could never ignore my mum. Besides, maybe it was preferable to be yelled at on the phone rather than being yelled at in person.

"Hello?" I answered.

"Is it true?" she asked.

I played dumb. "Is what true?"

She sighed. "I presume you've seen the news."

"I, uh, yeah… I have."

"So is it true?"

I groaned. "I mean, Mum, they have photos of us kissing, so of course it's kind of true. It's definitely written in a manipulative way, but yes, it's true."

"Well, I knew you kissed her, of course. That much is clear. I was hoping that was all it was. I was hoping that you did not sleep with that girl."

"I, uh…" I couldn't think of a more awkward conversation. "That's not all it was, Mother."

"Edward! I cannot believe you would take advantage of the staff in that way!"

"No, no, it wasn't like that, Mum! That was the one thing the article got incredibly wrong. I didn't take advantage of Maggie at all. She liked me… I mean, I hope she still likes me after this. She didn't feel pressured or anything, I'm positive she didn't. We had real feelings for each other."

My mum sighed. "That doesn't matter, Edward. I do not press you about the many vacations you take and what you do on them. I know I likely wouldn't approve of your behavior. You can gallivant around with any other woman in London, but you brought this into the palace. You brought it to an employee. I knew you and the young lady were friends, but I believed that was the extent of your relationship. I'm very, very disappointed in you, Edward."

I bit my lip. I hated hearing my mum tell me how upset she was.

"Mum, I get it, but I never thought of it that way. I didn't think it would reflect badly. I didn't think I was doing anything wrong."

"You're her boss, for crying out loud, Edward!" she continued.

"Well, no, not really. Sure, I was responsible for hiring her, but it wasn't like she reported to me or anything. Ms. Mitchell was her boss, and I told her that many times."

"So let me ask you, Edward," she continued. "Why did you hire her?"

"What?" I wasn't expecting that question.

"What reason did you have to hire her?"

"Well, she seemed like a good candidate, and—"

"And she was pretty?" my mum asked.

"I have always thought she was pretty, but I had other reasons for suggesting her."

"No, I don't think you really did. Which makes this entire situation so much worse. It makes it seem like you actually hired her to pursue her. You have to see how that looks in today's day and age. Male employers are constantly being called out for their sexual harassment."

"I never thought I was harassing her, not for a second! I mean, I wasn't harassing her! I truly wasn't. I care about her, Mother."

"I have to go, Edward. I have to figure out how we're going to handle this PR disaster. Please, don't speak to any journalists, don't agree to a single interview, and don't comment."

"Of course, Mum. I know the drill." I hated to feel my mother's disappointment, but I wasn't a child who needed to be scolded.

"I will talk to you when you get back," she said before hanging up.

Great, so I was going to get yelled at on the phone and in person. Perfect.

After speaking to my mum, I felt a lot worse. Not just because she was upset with me, but because what she was saying made a lot of sense. This truly would be a PR nightmare.

It looked bad on my part, I knew that. Though

maybe it would be curved by Maggie saying some nice things about me, clearing up our situation.

If she ever talked to me again. I couldn't be sure that she still had any interest in me after all this happened. This was exactly what she was worried about. It had come true, mostly because of my actions.

So I wasn't even sure if Maggie would come to my defense. Though, frankly, I wasn't sure I cared about that at the moment. I'd rather have her affection than her defense.

I told myself that despite all this, we still had a chance. Because that was the only thought that was going to get me through this. If we ended up together, I could handle the world's scrutiny. In fact, their opinions would mean nothing to me if I had Maggie by my side. Nobody could bother me. Until I knew I still had her, everything bothered me.

I tried to get my stuff together, pack up all my things so that I'd be prepared to leave tonight. Time dragged on with how stressed I was, and I decided to take a break. I had a good ten hours until I had to leave, so I needed to eat even if it was one of the last things on my mind.

I ordered some room service—just some fries because I didn't imagine I could stomach much more than that—and turned on the TV.

Of course, turning on the TV was a horrible idea, and I definitely should have known that. Front and center, as soon as the news came on, were photos of Maggie and me.

The news anchors were talking very seriously about whether my dating her was an abuse of power. They even brought an expert on workplace sexual harassment in to discuss it.

Bloody hell, this was a nightmare.

I wanted to flip the channels or turn the television off, but I couldn't bring myself to do it. It was like a train wreck. I didn't want to see it, but I couldn't peel my eyes away.

Room service knocked on the door and I went to open it, pulling out some cash to hand him as a tip; the food would have been put on a tab by the hotel.

"Hey, thanks a lot," I said, as I took the food

from him and handed him my cash.

When people run into me, I was used to getting a fairly positive reaction. This guy barely answered me.

"Uh-huh," he said with a disapproving glare.

Goddammit, had public opinion shifted this quickly?

Okay, I understood it. It was wrong to sleep with someone who worked for my family, but it was not at all abusive or coercive. She really liked me. We were growing toward a real relationship, not just some romp in the sheets.

I shut the door quickly behind him and put my food down. I no longer had any desire to eat it.

I reminded myself that I could deal with public opinion. That was bound to happen. I was in the spotlight, so I was going to be scrutinized. I grew up with that reality and was quite used to it. This was something that could be handled.

As long as Maggie wasn't done with me for exposing her. As long as there was still a chance with us, I'd be okay.

If there wasn't, I wasn't sure how I'd get through this.

It was a little hard for me to think about. I was starting to think this was the reason I'd fought commitment for so many years. It was so hard to feel as strongly as I did for Maggie and know that she may end things. That this may not work out for us. It felt like I was losing someone important to me, and after my father, I never wanted to lose anyone again. So I kept everybody at arm's length.

I just couldn't do that with Maggie. She sparked something in me. I felt drawn to her like a magnet, like it was impossible to do anything without her by my side.

Now I may have to face that possibility.

MCKENNA JAMES

Chapter 17

Maggie

"I just don't get it!" Abigail groaned.

"Well, let's go over it again. Okay, see, you almost got it, but that's a minus sign, not a plus sign." I was going over her math homework.

"Oh! I see!" She grinned. I loved the smile on her face whenever she finally understood something.

It was so rewarding to work with both kids, even though sometimes it felt like Drew didn't really need my help. He had his head buried in one of his Earth science books. I loved to be impressed by all the knowledge he constantly attained.

"My brother is supposed to come back today, you know," Abigail teased me.

She never let up on the idea that I had a crush on Edward. I mean, she wasn't wrong, but I never hinted that she was right about anything.

"Oh, that's great! I'm sure you're very excited

to see him." I played it off as if I didn't know already. I did, of course, and I was eager to talk to him about the hospital bill as well as put an end to this friends-with-benefits situation.

"I'm sure you're very excited to see him too." She kept teasing.

I rolled my eyes at Abigail but had to laugh at her persistence. Then Drew looked up from his book.

"Do you really like my brother?" he asked plainly. He wasn't joking at all, he genuinely wanted to know.

"Well, as a friend, of course I do," I told him.

"I don't mean as a friend," he clarified.

"Well, uh, no," I lied. "Your brother and I are just friends."

He looked disappointed, which was a reaction I wasn't expecting.

"What's wrong, Drew?"

"I just thought it would be nice if you liked him. Then you could come hang out at the palace even more."

That absolutely melted my heart.

Made what I had to do with Edward even harder.

It had to be done, I knew that. I couldn't keep putting it off, no matter how much I wanted to.

I wanted nothing more than to be part of this family. Even my anger towards Edward about the hospital bill eased a bit when I thought about being something real to him, an actual girlfriend.

That could not and would not happen. I had to start facing that head on. I would tonight.

Though that meant I'd only see Abigail and Drew in a professional capacity.

"Wait, okay, I'm confused again," Abigail said as she squinted at her math homework. Lord, that girl was adorable.

"Alright, let's take a look—"

Before I had a chance to, the door had opened, and someone walked in.

I recognized the woman, but I didn't know her name. I'd seen her around the palace frequently.

"Maggie?"

"Yes?" I asked.

"Ms. Mitchell would like to see you right away."

Drew and Abigail looked confused, so I made a joke for their benefit.

"Uh-oh, am I in trouble?"

The woman's face didn't ease. In fact, she looked significantly more serious. My heart dropped.

"Wait, am I actually in trouble?" I asked.

"Please, just follow me. Bring your things."

Bring my things?

I was so confused, but I did as she said. Surely I hadn't really done something wrong, right? I mean, what could I have even done?

I followed her down the hall and to a small office where Ms. Mitchell was sitting behind a desk.

"Please have a seat, Maggie," she instructed with a wave of her hand.

"Uh, I'm sorry, but I'm not sure what this is about," I told her, feeling like a dog with my tail tucked between my legs.

"I just have a few questions to ask you."

"Okay…"

I took my seat, my heart pounding in my chest. Ms., Mitchell was always a fairly serious woman, but there was something else in her attitude today. She seemed frustrated, maybe even mad at me. What on earth could I have done?

"Now, when I ask you this, I need you to be entirely honest with me. Do you understand?"

"Yes, of course," I agreed instantly.

"Have you had any relations with Prince Edward?"

I felt my face go flush with embarrassment. I wasn't sure what I was expecting, but it definitely wasn't that question.

"Uh, no, of course not," I lied without thinking, despite my insistence I'd be honest.

She sighed as she pulled something out of her desk drawer. She laid out in front of me a newspaper article with a large photo of Edward and me kissing.

I gasped. I couldn't believe what I was seeing. How was this the first time I was finding out about this? How did nobody text or call me about this?

Then I remembered that my phone didn't

charge last night, and I didn't notice until right before work. It had been running on very low battery. It probably died.

"Now, I'm going to ask you again—have you had any kind of relationship with Prince Edward?"

I looked down at my shoes, completely humiliated. "Yes, I have."

"Okay. Now, with that established, I must also ask—did you feel coerced in any way by the prince?"

"What?" This surprised me. "How do you mean?"

"Well, he was a superior to you after all. Did you feel he abused his power in any way to seduce you?"

"No!" I said quickly, without thinking. "That absolutely wasn't the case. Everything that happened between us was enthusiastically consensual." I felt embarrassed saying the words, but they needed to be said. "He absolutely did not coerce me."

She nodded and didn't say anything, but I thought I saw a flicker of relief cross her face.

"Alright, then. I am afraid I am going to have

to let you go."

"What?" I gasped. "I'm being fired?"

"Yes, unfortunately. I like you, Maggie. You are a sweet girl, and the kids love you. You have to understand how this reflects upon the royal family. We can't have you hired on if you intend to fraternize with Edward."

"I don't! I mean, I did, but... I was going to end it. Today, actually!"

"Even still, I'm afraid the queen is insistent that you cannot work within the palace anymore. Again, I am very sorry."

I was heartbroken. I knew there was nothing I could say to change her mind, so I stood and headed out of the office.

I didn't even get to say goodbye to the kids. Had I known this was going to happen, I could have talked to them about it, explained it to them...

Now when they found out, not only were they going to learn I'd never be coming back, but that I had lied to them about Edward and me. Their last memory of me was going to be of me being untruthful.

I felt like I was going to be sick.

This wasn't how I would have chosen to end things. I couldn't help but feel like I was abandoning the kids, even though I was the one being forced to leave. What was the difference to them, though? Whether I was forced to leave or left voluntarily, I was still effectively leaving them.

I wanted desperately to call someone, but who could I call? I had so few friends since my life was work and my father. I certainly couldn't call him.

Oh, no, but he probably already knew, didn't he? That was another thought that made my stomach turn. He was going to find out I was lying too. Ugh! He was going to be so disappointed in me when he learned I lost this job because I had a fling with the prince. It was such an important job to us.

Although I supposed after Edward paid for the hospital bills, it had become less important. Not to me. It still mattered for reasons outside of money.

I tried to think of who else I could talk to. Well,

Millie and I had become close, and she already kind of knew…

Then I pieced it together. Dammit, Millie knew! The day after she found out, this news breaks?

It had to be her who revealed us. Although some of those photos in the article were quite old… Maybe Millie reached out to some gossip journalist and they subsequently did some hunting. I wasn't sure exactly how that worked. I knew that if they had those photos months ago, they would've announced it.

I felt so stupid. I genuinely trusted her.

After how careful I was, after how nonchalant Edward was, I would've thought it was his actions that would have ultimately revealed us. I couldn't even be mad at him for this. It was only my actions that led us to this unfortunate predicament.

I decided to call Millie. I needed to know if it was her. I wanted to know if it truly was my fault that I was just fired.

I stopped in at a local coffee shop on my walk home. I wasn't exactly eager to go home anyway.

Even if my father hadn't heard the news already, he'd wonder why I was home early, and I'd have to explain. I'd put off going home as long as I possibly could.

I plugged my phone into the charger and waited impatiently for it to light up. As soon as it had, I dialed Millie.

At first, I thought she wasn't going to pick up. Which would only make me more suspicious of her… What other reason could she have for not answering me?

Right before it was about to go to voicemail, she answered.

"Hey, hun, what's up?" she answered in a perky tone. For a moment, I thought maybe I was being paranoid. She sounded pretty normal… Should I even accuse her of this?

I needed to. I needed to know. If it wasn't her, she would still understand why I had to ask.

"Hey, Millie. I was just calling because I wanted to talk to you about the other day. You know how you kind of figured things out about me and Edward?"

"Uh, yeah, I do. Why?"

"I was just wondering; did you tell anybody about that?"

"No, of course not." She tried to sound steady, but her voice cracked, and I knew instantly... She was lying to me.

Dammit.

"Don't lie to me, Millie. I only admitted to you this week that Edward and I had a tryst. You find out about us and days later, all this comes to light? Why? Why would you do this?"

She sighed dramatically before she replied, "I … I'm so sorry, Maggie. I wasn't going to do it, but then… Some things came up, and I really needed the money. I'd suspected you and Edward were messing around for weeks, I am the maid after all. I see and hear everything that happens within the walls of the palace." She tsked as if this bored her.

"You betrayed my trust!" I scolded.

"I wasn't entirely certain until you confessed to

me. Suddenly, I had a way to work through the financial struggles, and all my worries melted away. I hated to betray your confidence, but we're both from the same side of the track, Maggie. You'd have done the same if you were in my shoes. I didn't expect it would be a huge deal for you. You and Edward aren't even serious."

"Excuse me? It was an extremely big deal, Millie! I got fired today."

"You … what?" She seemed genuinely shocked. "Why?"

"Why do you think? It would reflect badly on the royal family for me to work for them after this scandal. I am without a job with an ailing father to care for, bills I can't possibly pay without income. You did that, Millie. You betrayed my trust, and what's worse—you admittedly did so. I considered you a friend, Millie. I'm so hurt that you would throw our friendship away without care."

"I'm so, so sorry, Maggie. I didn't think that you would get fired. I thought since the only source was what I told them, they'd make up some gossipy article that didn't confirm anything and people would brush it off. I didn't know they were going to find the pictures. I didn't think it was going to be so concrete."

"Well, it was. My life is drastically different because of it."

"Maggie, I can't apologize to you enough. I'm so very sorry that you lost your job. I was just desperate and did a horrible thing, but I don't regret making the choice I had to make to benefit my needs. Surely you can understand that?"

Actually, I could understand that. I'd been pretty desperate in the situation with my father.

I didn't want to give Millie any sympathy right now. She was trying to justify her actions, which I completely disagreed with. Maybe if I wasn't just fired, I'd be able to respond with a more clarity, but right now, I simply couldn't do it.

"Goodbye, Millie," I said before hanging up.

"No, wait! Maggie, wait!"

It was too late. I'd shut the phone down. I didn't want to hear anything more from her.

I tried to hold it together in the coffee shop, but it was easier said than done. I was distraught.

I wondered if Edward knew about any of this yet. We definitely wouldn't be meeting up later after my shift…

That was when it hit me. I'd never be going back to the palace ever again. I could feel tears welling up in my eyes, and I rushed out of the coffee shop and started my walk home.

My very slow walk home. Because I wasn't looking forward to explaining this to my father.

Though at least I could finally tell him about the hospital bills being paid off by Edward. I'd been delaying because I didn't know how to explain Edward's generosity. Well, there was no hiding the reason now, so he might as well know.

Maybe that bit of information would soften the blow.

Chapter 18

Edward

Maggie hadn't answered any of my calls. I didn't bother trying to call once I got off the plane because I knew she'd be working with Abigail and Drew. I didn't want to bother her. I'd see her soon enough at the end of her shift.

I went to the tutoring room and waited outside the door, feeling a little nauseated as I considered what I'd say to her. Each minute ticked by so slowly.

When the final minute ticked by and the teachers began to file out of the room, I thought I might actually throw up.

Except, she never came out of the room. All the other educators did, and they shot me disapproving glances along the way, but Maggie wasn't there.

I was so confused. Did she not come into work today? Was the news that bad to her?

I stepped into the room, rather lost in thought,

but when I heard the chair scrape the marble floor, I looked up and immediately knew what had happened.

"Where's Maggie?" I asked immediately.

Ms. Mitchell sighed. "I had to let her go, Edward."

"Let her go? Why? She didn't do anything wrong!" I argued, although I knew this would be a consequence.

This was horrible news. She didn't deserve to be fired. She was great with the kids. They loved her. She loved this job.

She must be absolutely livid with me if my spontaneous behavior got her fired.

"Of course she did something wrong. She wasn't supposed to date you."

"But it was all me!" I argued. "I pursued her! I went after her. You can't fire her for that."

"That's very honorable for you to try to take the blame," Ms., Mitchell said, "but she made it very clear to me that she took as much interest in you as you took in her. You are both equally to blame."

"If we're equally to blame, we should have equal consequences. I don't have any consequences!" I said angrily.

"Oh, Edward," she said in frustration. "If you think you have no consequences, you are not paying attention to the media. You have a great many consequences, and I fear they are more serious than her being fired. Have you seen what they're saying about you? You come off as a predator."

"I don't care about that." I slapped the desk with my hand. "I care about Maggie. I care that what I've done has hurt her."

"It's what you both have done," Ms. Mitchell reminded me. "I cannot help you, Edward. I will be the first to admit I am quite fond of Maggie. She was always a great tutor, but the queen insists she cannot continue to work here, and frankly, I agree with her."

"That's absurd, Ms. Mitchell, and you know it," I groaned. "All my life it's been preached of the importance of finding my soul mate, a princess who would one day accept the throne as queen. Now that I'm confident I've found that in Maggie, you strip her from my life?"

Ms. Mitchell looked at me curiously. "You actually care for this girl, don't you?" she asked.

"Yes, of course I do. Is it not obvious?" I threw my arms out wide, the frustration for the situation, my heart on my sleeve, both on full display.

"It's just that I've never seen you so up in arms over any woman before. It's quite a shock."

"Well, I'm smitten. I really am. Head over heels in love with her. What more can I say?"

She paused, seeming to think for a moment.

"You know, the queen probably would not appreciate me giving you this advice, but..." she began hesitantly.

"What? What is it? Please, Ms. Mitchell, I'm at your mercy," I pleaded.

"If you truly care for this girl, if you want to mitigate her pain, I would seek her out. You cannot give her the job back, but I do not believe the job will be the most important thing to her right now."

I was shocked that Ms. Mitchell was actually encouraging me to pursue Maggie.

"Really? You think I should go to her?"

"I absolutely do."

I smiled despite the awful situation.

"Edward, never before have I seen you head-over-heels for a woman. This kind of affection, it's rare. Take it from an old woman. You have to chase that feeling once it comes over you. So, go chase her while you still can."

I nodded. "Thank you, Ms. Mitchell."

"You're absolutely welcome."

I tried calling Maggie as soon as I left the palace to let her know I was coming over right away. She didn't answer, but I didn't care. I was going to go whether she answered or not. I absolutely had to talk to her.

I had my driver rush over. He wouldn't speed for me, despite my best begging for him to do so, and every minute dragged on. Once her flat came into view, I was ready to jump out of the car.

I ran across the grass and up to her door. I knocked on it impatiently, praying that she was here. She had to be, right? Where else would she be? She spent much of her time with her father.

The door opened, and my heart pounded in my chest as I hoped to see her face. I didn't see her face. I saw a man's face.

"Hello?" he said as he opened the door.

"Hello, you must be Maggie's father," I said quickly, a little out of breath from running to the door.

"Yes. And you are…? Wait." He paused, and his eyes widened. "You're … the prince?"

"I am." I smiled politely.

"Oh my. Come in! Come in!" he said, and he took me by the arm. "I can't believe the Prince of England is at my door. Please, make yourself at home. It's not much, but I hope it's comfortable."

I looked around the flat. It was simple but tastefully decorated. "I think it's quite nice actually," I said politely.

This seemed to flatter him. "Ah, well, I take it you're looking for Maggie, right? She's just in her room. Let me go fetch her."

"Thank you very much," I told him.

He was bald and frail, but he seemed to be getting around alright. Maggie had described him as needing a lot of help, so I could only hope his mobility was a sign that his health was improving.

I sat on their couch as I waited. It was quaint, and I actually quite liked it. Having always grown up in extravagance, I wasn't used to this.

It reminded me of the shows I used to watch as a child, sitcoms with entirely normal families. I used to be so jealous growing up, so desperate for an average house in a normal neighborhood. Most people would likely think that ridiculous, but luxury stops feeling luxurious when you're constantly surrounded by it. At least, that was how it worked for me.

I heard footsteps coming from down the hall, and I straightened up on the couch.

Out came Maggie. Her eyes were red and puffy, she'd definitely been crying. It broke my heart to see her this way.

"Maggie, I am truly sorry."

"For what?" she asked.

This seemed like a weird question considering

our circumstance.

"For everything that's happened, of course."

"You mean with me being outed as your lover and fired?" she questioned.

"Yes," I answered nervously.

"That's not what you should be sorry for."

She sat on an armchair across the way from me and stared on blankly.

"Uh ... then I really haven't a clue what I should be sorry for."

"I know about the hospital bill," she answered seriously.

Wait; that was what she was mad about? I thought she'd be thrilled!

"Did I do something wrong?"

"I'm not a charity case, Edward. I can fend for myself. That was a really big gesture you made, and I don't think you considered how it was going to make me feel."

"I don't think you're a charity case at all! Maggie, I didn't do it to provide you charity."

"So why did you do it? Because to me it feels

like maybe it was some kind of bribe. Like you wanted to thank me for all the sex or—"

"Woah, woah, woah! Let's slow down here. I absolutely wasn't trying to manipulate you. I didn't pay off the hospital bills in trade for sex. Maggie, I did it because I am in love with you, and the thought of you struggling with hospital bills while also taking care of your father was breaking my heart. You were already doing so much, and I didn't think you deserved to have anything else on your plate, especially when I could've taken care of it easily."

She was quiet as she processed this, so I continued.

"Look, I can see why you were upset. Yes, I should have asked. I definitely shouldn't have done it without your consent first. I didn't think it through. I honestly thought you'd be relieved to have one less thing to worry about. In my slight defense, I was concussed at the time."

"Really? You decided when you had the concussion?"

"Actually, that is why I got concussed in the

first place. While playing polo, I couldn't get you out of my mind. I'd battled with myself about if this was real—if you were the one. No other woman sparks emotion in me like you do." She swiped away at a tear and struggled to find her breath. "I decided the very moment I was whopped upside the head, effectively resulting in the concussion. Even as I lay in the grass, dizzy and barely coming to, I couldn't get you out of my head. I decided right then to pay the hospital bills, and I called my lawyer the next day."

"But why?" she asked, puzzled.

"I ... I don't think I understand the question. Isn't it obvious?"

"No, it's not obvious to me at all. It's the exact opposite of obvious. Why would you care so much about what I'm going through? Why would the woman you're sleeping with be that important to you? We were nothing more but a fling. Friends with benefits."

"Is that all you think you are?! The woman I'm sleeping with?!" I was appalled.

"Aren't I?"

"Maggie, you are so much more than that to me. I am in love with you. Simply put. I can't even explain how much. You've become a best friend to me."

Finally, for the first time today, a small smile formed on her face.

She quickly forced it away.

"You're in love with me?" She seemed stunned beyond belief.

I grabbed her cheeks and kissed her breathless. "Yes, woman. You're maddening."

"Maybe I overreacted about the hospital bill. I do forgive you for that, and I do appreciate it... But—"

"You don't forgive me for word getting out about us?" I finished for her.

"What? No. That wasn't what I was going to say at all. In fact, I'm pretty sure it wasn't your fault."

I raised an eyebrow. "How can that be? I was the one who was careless. You were constantly saying we should be more discrete."

"Yes, well, all that aside, I'm still the reason

word of our situation got out."

"How could you possibly know that?"

"Well, uh, I may have been really mad at you when I found out about the hospital bill, so I vented to Millie about it, and I accidentally said too much. I never explicitly said we had done anything together, but she figured it out."

"You're sure she was the one to leak it?"

"Yep, I called her afterward, and she confirmed it."

I could feel my face flush with anger.

"How dare she?! I'm going to have her fired promptly. And to think, she acted like your friend!"

"No, no, please don't do that," Maggie instantly begged.

I couldn't understand why.

"You just said that she outed us?"

"I know. On the phone, she sounded pretty desperate and apologetic, although she attempted to justify her actions as if that made everything better. She did it because she was stressed about money and, well, I can definitely understand that. If you fire her, she will only be more stressed."

I never ceased to be amazed by Maggie's compassion. She was truly an amazing being.

"That's incredibly kind of you."

She shrugged. "I just don't see why anyone should experience any more pain because of what has happened. What's done is done. I just want to move forward."

"Okay, so, if you're not mad at me about the hospital bill and you're not mad at Millie... What are you mad at?" I asked.

"I'm not at all."

"But there was a but. You said you forgave me 'but?'"

"Right. I forgive you, but we can't be together."

"What?! But why?"

"Because as fun as this fling is between us, Edward, I'm not the kind of girl who can have a fling and not get attached. I wanted to end things a long time ago for that reason, but I couldn't pluck up the courage to do it. Well, now I'm doing it. I can't keep sleeping with you without wanting something more."

"So then… Why can't we have something more? I just told you I love you, Maggie. Why are you complicating things?" I asked. That was what I wanted after all.

"You know why, Edward. We could never be together in this world. Who am I? I'm a total nobody. I'm not the kind of woman you can date. You need to date someone higher up in society. Someone who can live up to being a princess."

"You absolutely live up to being a princess, Maggie."

She blushed. "Edward, you know what I mean. I'm not the woman for you long term. You could never marry someone like me. It wouldn't be right. So let's end this before it hurts too much."

"No, Maggie. You deserve to see your worth, and you're worth it all to me," I argued.

"Edward…"

"Maggie, I am not going to let you go. I can't. I don't care if people don't think you're the kind of woman who should become princess. I don't care what anyone thinks because the only opinion that matters to me is yours. I want to be true to myself. I don't want to be what people expect me to be. Being true to myself means being with you."

She looked up at me expectantly. "Do you really mean that? You really want to be with me?"

"Absolutely!" I slid over on the couch so I could reach out and grab her hand. "Maggie, I may not be able to make them hire you back at the palace, but I can certainly let the world know that you're my girlfriend. If you agree to be that is."

A grin broke out on her face as she nodded furiously.

"Yes, yes, of course I'll be your girlfriend!" she chimed.

It was music to my ears.

I leaned in and kissed her passionately. Except not too passionately because I was painfully aware that her father could walk in at any moment.

"So, I'm in the official girlfriend role, huh?" she asked.

"Sure are."

"Does that come with a t-shirt or something? 'I went to the palace and all I got was this lousy boy-friend?'"

I had to laugh. "I can have one made, if you want."

"Yes, I'd like that," she joked.

I loved that she was lightening the mood. It put me at ease once again.

"Have you two love birds patched things up?" I looked up to find Maggie's dad standing in the hall-way. So he must have heard about us in the news as well.

"Uh ... yeah, actually, we have." Maggie stood. "Dad, I want you to meet my boyfriend, Ed-ward."

I loved the way she said that. It was so casual. In that moment, I didn't feel like the Prince of Eng-land. I felt like any average guy meeting his girl-friend's father. I adored the fact that Maggie gave me a sense of normalcy that I had never had before.

"Well, lovely to meet you, Edward."

He extended his hand for me to shake, and I

shook it proudly.

Maggie looked absolutely delighted.

"I'm going to grab us some drinks. I think this calls for a celebration," she said as she scurried off to the kitchen, leaving me and her father alone.

Just like any average guy meeting his girl-friend's father, I was suddenly a bit intimidated.

He was nice enough. He took a seat next to me on the couch.

"Sir, I know that this is going to come off as … a little premature," I began to say to him, "but there is something I want to ask you." I didn't know when I might get the opportunity to be alone with him again, and I had to capitalize on it.

"Yes?" he asked.

"I was wondering if I could get your blessing to propose to your daughter, when the time is right?"

His eyes widened. "You want to marry her?"

"I do, with all my heart. I know it's early, but there is never going to be a woman out there for me who isn't Maggie. She's made me feel whole from the moment she entered my life, and I can't imagine my world without her in it."

He looked at me seriously. "You really love her, huh?"

"With every piece of myself."

He nodded slowly. "You have my blessing, but you have to promise me one thing."

"What? Anything," I responded.

"You have to take care of my girl. She's a special one. She hasn't let the world make her hard. Being with you means experiencing a lot of negativity from the world. You must protect her from all that."

"I promise. I will care for her above all else. She will forevermore be my biggest priority."

He smiled. "Then yes, you can certainly ask my daughter to marry you."

Chapter 19

Maggie

Both my father and I were glued to the television screen as we waited for Edward's press conference to start.

Frankly, I had no idea what Edward was going to say. He hadn't detailed it for me. He only teased me that I had to tune in to find out.

The past week with him had been absolutely amazing, a dream come true. Some mornings, I still woke up and wondered if it was all a dream. Surely, I couldn't be the girlfriend of the Prince of England?

I was.

It was a lot to adjust to in my mind. After the initial excitement wore off, I had to deal with all the nervousness of what people were going to think. Particularly, I was worried about the opinion of the Queen. I knew that she was quite hard on Edward and had high expectations, and it didn't seem that I would fit her standards.

According to Edward, though, she was really understanding about the situation. He explained to her that he cared for me deeply and that it was a serious relationship, and she acquiesced. She even asked to meet with me yesterday evening which was stressful, but ultimately it ended up going very well. We had tea, and she asked me about my life. I think she really liked me.

I was relieved to have Edward tell me about how Ms. Mitchell responded to learning he cared for me. Apparently, she encouraged him to seek me out. I'd always be grateful to her for that. Not that Edward wouldn't have sought me out on his own. I believed nothing would've kept him from announcing his true feelings for me.

I was still upset that I lost my job, but frankly, being with Edward eased that pain considerably. Now that I was with him, I knew that I'd always be part of Drew and Abigail's life. In fact, if we ever did get married (fingers crossed) I'd become their sister-in-law.

They say when you marry someone, you marry their whole family. Well, despite not wanting to be in the spotlight, this was one family I was really happy to marry into.

I was getting ahead of myself, though. I couldn't be sure that Edward and I would end up marrying. We barely started dating! We were a long way off from that.

Still, it was hard for me to imagine ever ending up with anybody else. Edward was amazing. He was all I'd ever wanted. I'd be heartbroken if we ever had to end things.

Suddenly, the press conference came on the screen, and I was on the edge of my seat.

"Hello, everyone, thank you for coming. I called this press conference today to discuss the information about my love life that has been spiraling across the media. There are a few things I'd like to clear up."

He cleared his throat.

"First of all, yes, I did have a relationship with my younger siblings' tutor. I assure everyone, this was not a relationship that developed out of coercion. On the contrary, Maggie was very serious about her attraction to me just as I am serious about her. I am excited to inform everyone that we are officially dating, she is my girlfriend."

I swooned. I couldn't believe that he had just claimed me as his girlfriend for all of England. It was such a beautiful thing to hear. It was another one of those 'pinch me' moments. I couldn't process that this was my life.

"I understand that it is inappropriate for me to seriously date anyone on the royal staff and because of this, she is no longer employed with the royal family. I am genuinely apologetic for the way our relationship started, though I am not at all apologetic to be with her. Maggie is my one true love, and if I had to suffer all this bad press again to be with her, I'd do it in a heartbeat."

Tears were welling in my eyes, and my dad patted me gently on the back.

"That boy, he's a keeper, my dear. He truly is."

I nodded. He was absolutely right. Edward was

incredibly special.

"At this time, I will be fielding your questions," Edward announced.

I didn't get a chance to listen to the first question because somebody had rung my doorbell.

"I'll get it!" My dad jumped up.

"No, no, sit and rest... I've got it," I assured him, though he had been quite active lately. He seemed to be doing much better.

"Don't you want to watch the rest of the press conference?" he asked.

"You sit and watch," I insisted, "you can fill me in."

I walked to the door. I expected it was a mail delivery and was entirely shocked to find Edward standing before me.

"But ... wait," I paused, "how can you be here when you're there?" I pointed to the TV stupidly.

He laughed, "The press conference wasn't live, Maggie."

"Oh, I thought it was..." I felt a little stupid.

"Can I come in?"

"Yeah, yeah, of course. Come on."

He walked in and immediately greeted my father. "So nice to see you again."

"And lovely to see you, Edward. What brings you here today?"

"Well, actually, I wanted to invite Maggie on a vacation."

I raised an eyebrow. "A vacation? I thought your party days were over now."

He laughed. "It isn't that kind of vacation. It'll be a very calm vacation. A relaxing tropical trip. Do you get seasick?"

"I, uh, have no idea," I answered honestly. I'd never been on a boat.

"Well, pack a bathing suit and some cool clothing because we leave tonight if you're willing."

"I'm not so sure I am." I looked over at my father and then back at Edward. "I shouldn't leave my dad for a whole week."

"Nonsense!" my father piped up. "You haven't had a proper vacation since I became sick. You need this, Maggie, and I've been feeling very good as of late."

"What if I have a caretaker come over for the duration of our trip? For the time that you would normally be around? Would that be okay with both of you?" Edward looked to me and then my father.

I turned to my father too.

"Of course that would be fine!" he said eagerly.

Then Edward looked expectantly toward me.

"Well…" I hesitated a bit, "if it's really okay with my dad, I suppose I can go."

Edward gave me a respectful kiss on the cheek. "Fantastic! Let's go get you packed!" He put his hand on my back and walked me into my room.

I closed the door behind us for some privacy. I knew my father wouldn't mind.

"So, did you watch the press conference?" he asked.

"I did. It was really sweet the way you talked about me."

"Not too mushy?" he asked.

I sat next to him on the bed. "Not too mushy at all."

We kissed for a moment, but it wasn't a sexual kiss. It was sweet, quick, just to express that we appreciated each other's company.

"You have no idea how happy I am that you agreed to be my girlfriend. I can't help but shout it from the rooftops. This should technically be the most stressful time of my life, being that it's my first scandal and all, but it's really not with you by my side. I feel like I can take on anything with you."

I leaned into him. "I feel the exact same way. I never imagined I'd have a chance with you."

He laughed. "Funny, because I thought you were out of my league from the beginning."

Me? Out of his league? He was set to be the King of England, for crying out loud!

I didn't argue. I loved that he always made me feel special and important.

"You know, for all your fussing about it, I think you're going to make a great Queen."

I chuckled. "Oh, stop! Now your flattery is really going too far."

"But it's not at all!" he insisted.

"What reason could you possibly have to think I'd be a good queen?"

He didn't even have to think about his answer. "The way you responded to Millie. It was very empathetic, considerate, and diplomatic. Anyone else would have probably insisted on her being fired. Not you. Because you're different, Maggie, you're something special."

I smiled and leaned into his chest. He wrapped his arms around me.

"You know, a wise woman once told me that to help with my responsibilities as King, I should find a woman who would be a good guide for me. I'm pretty sure I have."

He kissed the top of my head, and I just about melted.

I cleared my throat, unsure how to respond to such a huge compliment.

"So where exactly is it that we're going?" I asked.

"Oh, you'll see. I think you're going to love it. It's calm, luxurious … everything you need after all

275

the stress we've been through recently."

"Mmm… Sounds nice. Though, honestly, I think anywhere I'm with you is calm and luxurious."

"I couldn't agree more."

Chapter 20

Edward

I left Maggie to pack her things for a few hours and told her I'd return with a car to take us to our flight. I was very ambiguous about the whole thing, so she likely thought we were taking a plane somewhere.

We weren't. We were actually going to take a helicopter to fly us to a private yacht.

I hoped this vacation would be perfect for her. I'd gone to great lengths to organize every detail and had even thrown in a few surprises along the way.

It was going to be extravagant, but I felt Maggie deserved it.

In the week that had passed since I made Maggie my girlfriend officially, I had been happier than I could ever remember being. It was as if there'd been a missing puzzle piece in my life for so long, and I wasn't even aware of it. She had filled in all the gaps of my life.

The sense of loneliness I struggled for years had dissipated. I felt less lonely sitting in an empty room with her than I did with a crowd of people. I had come to realize that despite filling my space with a people I thought I liked, I had nobody who really understood me or fulfilled me.

I knew that it was crazy to say I knew this woman was meant to be my wife, but that was true. I felt it in my soul. I knew that Maggie was the one for me. There was no doubt in my mind.

Admittedly, when I brought up the proposal to my mother, she was hesitant. She didn't believe I'd marry anytime soon and assumed when I did, I'd have spent more than a few months with the woman.

It took a lot of convincing, but I begged her to give Maggie a fair chance. I insisted I was going to propose soon, regardless of her opinion, of course, but I really wanted her to get along fully with Maggie.

After we all spent an evening together, I realized my mother getting along with Maggie would be no issue. She adored her. She saw in her what I always had. She was intelligent, kind, eloquent—everything that a prince's wife should be.

I didn't care what a prince's wife should be, however. I only cared that I loved her with my whole heart. I knew my mother did care, though, and it was nice that she was impressed.

Of course, my siblings loved Maggie as well. That much had always been clear. Though they were a bit confused at first when I announced our relationship to them, they quickly adjusted and were gloriously happy. It had been hard on them to learn that they were losing Maggie as a tutor, however it made things much easier to hear that they were gaining her as a sister-in-law.

In my mind, it was a great sign for my decision to marry her (and quickly) that she assimilated so easily into my family. Likewise, I had already come to like her father quite a bit.

I had not voiced this to neither Maggie nor her father, but secretly I was glad to have a father figure in my life. Not that anyone could ever replace my father. It felt good to know that my future children would have a grandfather in their life. They wouldn't be missing out on anything because I lost my dad.

It seemed serendipitous that both Maggie and I were gaining the parents we had lost.

As my driver pulled up outside of Maggie's flat, I got out of the car to fetch her. I hoped she would be packed by now. I had my own bags in the back of the car.

Normally, I'd have somebody else load up Maggie's luggage in the car, but I wanted to do it myself. Being around Maggie, I often felt like a normal guy. I had been feeding into that as often as possible. I knew I was still a Prince, still had a great responsibility, and a lot of fame, but I'd take any little moments of normalcy that I could get.

I knocked on her door, and she answered quickly, a suitcase in hand.

"Is that all you have?" I asked as I looked at her floral mint suitcase.

"Of course. We're only going for a week,

right?"

"Right."

I was a little embarrassed of my three suitcases now. Perhaps I didn't quite know how to live like the average person yet. I was sure, over the years, Maggie would teach me. Just as I'd teach her to adjust to being royal. I hoped we'd always have the best of both worlds.

"So, do I get to know where we're going yet?" she asked.

"No, of course not," I said as I opened the car door for her and took her suitcase to the back.

I climbed in the car next to her. She sat in the middle seat and after I buckled myself in, I put my arm around her.

"So, are we going to a public airport or is this some kind of chartered flight?" she asked. "How do the rich and famous travel?"

"I suppose you'll find out, won't you?"

"You're seriously not going to give me anything?!" She groaned as she leaned her head on my shoulder.

"Trust me, it'll be better if you're surprised. I'd like to shock you on this vacation."

"Probably won't be hard to do considering I've gone on like, two vacations in my life... Neither of which were particularly fancy."

"Yeah? And, where were they?"

"Well, the first was to Disneyland when I was a kid. And my mom and dad saved for a year to get me there. Then the second was on my senior trip to London. That was when I decided I wanted to study abroad. I fell in love with everything about London. I knew I didn't want to live in America again if I could avoid it."

"Ah, I get it now." I looked at her skeptically.

"What?" she asked.

"You're marrying a royal for the easy citizenship, aren't you?"

She laughed. "Actually, it was for the great healthcare."

We both chuckled as we approached the helipad where a helicopter was already waiting for us. Maggie didn't even notice it at first, but when the car stopped, she looked over to her right and her jaw dropped.

"Wait... Are you kidding me?! We're not taking a plane."

"Nope. Hope that's alright with you."

"Alright with me?! Traveling by helicopter?! Uh, yeah, I think I can live with that." She laughed as she gleefully jumped out of the car before I could even open the door.

I loved how overtly excited she got about every little thing I introduced her to. Other women I'd been with seemed to go to great lengths to not seem overly impressed. I could only imagine this was a show of status. They wanted to appear as if this lifestyle was mundane to them, like they belonged in it. Perhaps they even believed it would make me fall for them, as if they were showing they'd adjust to the royal lifestyle easily.

Nothing could appeal to me less. Everything that attracted me to Maggie stemmed from her ambivalence to this life. The way she didn't even recognize me when we first met, that drew me to her like nothing else.

We stepped into the helicopter, and I got her set up with protective gear. We buckled in and the entire ride, glee never left her face. She was totally amazed. We could barely speak to each other over the sound of the helicopter whirring, but she would nudge me and point down at the ground below us often.

It would be impossible to continue to take the luxuries of my life for granted with Maggie around. Everything I'd grown used to, she found such joy in. It forced me to find the joy in it as well.

We landed at another helipad that was near to the yacht that we'd be traveling on. Even though we were by the ocean, Maggie didn't at first realize what our trip was.

"Oh, are we going on a cruise?!" she asked excitedly.

I had to laugh.

"I can't go on a cruise, Maggie. I'd never get any peace or quiet. We are going out on a boat, though... A yacht, to be exact."

This excited her even more. "Really?! Just the two of us?"

"Something like that." I smiled mischievously.

She looked at me skeptically but didn't question it further. Likely because she was too thrilled to learn about the plan.

Good, that meant she'd be even more surprised.

This time, I allowed staff from the yacht to come collect our things. I wanted Maggie to have the full experience. She did seem to enjoy this a bit as I walked onto the yacht with her.

"So, what all can we do on this yacht?" she asked.

"Well, it has a small pool, a hot tub, a game room, a very beautiful dining hall with a premiere cooking staff..."

She was glowing. "I can't believe you're taking me on a trip like this so soon!" She hugged me tightly. "Thank you. I really needed this."

"I know you did." I kissed her forehead. "I hope that you know you deserve every second of this trip, Maggie. I know how hard you've worked, how much energy you've put into caring for your father. You deserve to relax. In fact, this vacation won't even do all the work you've done justice. Though I hope it helps."

I could see tears welling up in her eyes before she leaned up to kiss me passionately. When she pulled away, she wiped her eyes.

"You have no idea what it means to me to hear that. Thank you. I don't think I even realized how badly I needed all my efforts validated until now."

"You're very welcome," I said as I looked around. They should have been here by now...

"What is it?" she asked, immediately noticing my confusion. I wished she couldn't read my emotions so easily.

"Oh, nothing, just looks different from when I used this charter last time. Perhaps a different yacht."

"Maybe."

I pulled out my phone and texted my mother.

>>We're here on the deck. Where are you and the kids?

>>So sorry, just arrived, coming down right now.

My heart was pounding in my chest. For a moment, nerves took over me. I knew I wanted to do this and trusted it was the right decision but still, I knew it was hasty. I feared that maybe Maggie wasn't going to feel the same way that I did. Perhaps she'd think it too early.

Still, I had to ask, I had to know. I couldn't wait another day.

I saw Abigail and Drew shuffling down the runway, and I smiled at Maggie.

"What is it?" she questioned.

I took her hands in mine.

"Maggie, I have something I need to ask you."

"Okay..." she said hesitantly.

"Getting to know you these past few months has easily been the best time of my life. Before you, I didn't know what love was, didn't even have a clue. I thought all that love-at-first-sight nonsense was just for romantic comedies. The day you spilled coffee on me, I felt something special. I've been drawn to you

287

ever since. I am so glad that I not only had the opportunity to meet you but to make you my girlfriend."

She smiled. "I'm so glad too, Edward, but... Why are you saying all this?"

"Because there is only one thing in this world that I can imagine will be more magical than making you my girlfriend."

"What's that?"

"Making you my wife."

Before she could even answer, I put my hands on her shoulders and slowly turned her around so that she was facing Abigail and Drew.

She squealed when she saw them and subsequently yelled out even louder when she saw the sign they were both holding onto that read: 'Will you marry me, Maggie?'

When she turned around to me, there were tears in her eyes, and her hands had flung to her mouth in shock.

I knelt down before her, took the extravagant diamond ring out of my pocket, and presented it to her.

"Will you be my wife?"

"Yes!" she screamed out. "Yes, yes, of course I will!"

I quickly got off of one knee, picked her up, and twirled her around wildly. Before she even took the ring out of the box to try on, she turned toward the kids. It was another reminder of why I loved her so dearly. Material possessions would always come second to her when family was around.

"I can't believe you two are here! I can't believe you were able to help with this!" She scooped them up and hugged them tightly.

"You're gonna be our sister now!" Abigail said excitedly.

"I sure am!" She turned to Drew and ruffled his hair.

"Welcome to the family." He grinned.

"Yes, welcome to the family." I heard a voice from behind me.

It was my mother's, and she was smiling warmly at the both of us.

"A truly beautiful proposal Edward, congratulations." She took me in her arms and kissed my cheek.

Then she turned her affection to Maggie, pulling her in for a tight hug.

"It will be truly wonderful to have another daughter."

I smiled at my family before me. On this yacht, I had the most important people in my life. To have them here as I celebrated easily the biggest moment of my life… It meant so much to me.

Finally, I took Maggie's hand and slid the ring onto her finger. She stared at it, wide-eyed.

"It is incredibly gorgeous, Edward, thank you!"

"Not nearly as beautiful as you."

I hugged her tight and then kissed her. For the first time, I was kissing the lips of my fiancée.

It felt so good.

Chapter 21

Maggie

I stared down at my finger as the light from the window hit it gently. It was amazing how every time sunlight splashed upon it, it lit up like a fire. I loved the way it twinkled.

It was weird because I'd never been one to take a particular interest in jewelry. I never thought I'd come to care about a diamond.

Really, it wasn't the diamond I cared about. It was the reminder that I was now an engaged woman that meant so much to me.

I still couldn't believe it. Just weeks ago, I was still in awe that I was Edward's girlfriend. Now I was going to be his wife?

I tried to imagine what that would mean. The wife of the Prince of England… Well, I'd never have to worry about money again, that was for sure. Which meant that I'd never again fret over a hospital bill.

Although, I was hoping not to have to worry about hospital bills for other reasons. I just got a call from my father yesterday, and he shared with me that at his last doctor appointment, they declared him cancer-free! He was now in remission!

Of course, that didn't mean it would stay that way. I understood just how brutal cancer could be. At any time, it could return. At least if it did, he would get the absolute best care in the country thanks to Edward.

Aside from that, being with Edward afforded me the luxury of doing whatever I wanted in life. I could pursue my passions, whatever those were.

Huh, weird, I truly didn't know what my passions were. I supposed I'd been so involved with taking care of my father and working for so long that I didn't have time to consider what I wanted for my life.

I tried to think of what made me happy, besides Edward of course, and only one thing came to mind...

Children. Watching Abigail and Drew grow

was the most rewarding time of my life. They made me so incredibly happy.

Perhaps that was what I wanted for my future—children. Yes, as I thought it, I knew that was it. I wanted to be a mother.

I stared out the window of the yacht as I considered it. Edward would make a wonderful father. I'd seen firsthand how amazing he was with his siblings. I had no doubts he'd be just as amazing with our own children.

"What are you thinking about?" I heard his voice say from behind me.

I turned around. He had just come out of the bathroom, a towel wrapped around his waist. I admired the way the water dripped from his chest down to his abs.

"Children," I answered honestly.

Perhaps I shouldn't have. Saying that I was thinking about kids was coming along a little strong. It was the truth. I never wanted to lie to Edward.

Besides, could you really come on too strong to your future husband?

"Children like … your own future children?"

"Yep!" I smiled. "Does that scare you?"

"Not at all," he said as he walked toward the bed. "In fact, I'm excited by the idea."

"Really?" I asked. "You want kids?"

"Yep, tons of them. You know, I hear they're kind of hard to make."

I looked at him skeptically. "What on earth are you talking about?"

"Children, they're hard to make! So, you know, we should probably spend a little time practicing."

Now I understood his point. "Oh, yeah? You think so?"

"Absolutely."

He climbed into bed with me. Even if I wanted to deny him, I couldn't. He was too damn hot.

Not that I'd denied him since we'd become engaged. I was most certainly in the honeymoon stage, and if this yacht wasn't so luxurious, I might never leave the room.

At least we had some time before brunch.

He began to kiss at my neck, and instantly I was breathing quicker. You'd think eventually I'd get used to something as simple as neck kisses, but I never seemed to.

As he kissed, he began to pull my pants down, exposing my lace panties. He managed to do this without ever pulling his mouth away from my neck.

Slowly, he started rubbing the outside of my panties. That combined with the neck kissing already had me wet enough to get started, and I'd be lying if I said I wasn't already craving his cock.

I let him continue with the foreplay because I was eager to make this last as long as possible.

I reached down and grabbed his towel, pulling it off him in one fluid motion. My eyes were quickly drawn to his rock-hard cock that was now dangling in front of him. It brushed up against my leg, and it took all the willpower I had not to beg him to jam it in me.

To soothe my craving for him, I instead reached down and grabbed his shaft. I heard him moan gently against my neck as he felt me touch his manhood, but he didn't stop kissing me.

Slowly, I started rubbing my hand up and down his shaft. As I did, his neck kisses became more intense. He wasn't just kissing me anymore; he was biting me.

Fuck, I loved it when he got rough.

He let his hand slide up to my panty line, and then he hooked a finger around the waist of my panties and pulled them down so that my bare pussy was exposed. I took in a deep breath as his finger found my clit.

He finally pulled away from my neck and looked down at me. I was wearing nothing now but my button-down pajama top which he promptly ripped off my body. It sent a few buttons flying, but I truly didn't care. Lord knew we could afford more pajamas.

Now my breasts were exposed along with my pussy, and he turned his attention to them instead of my neck. Slowly, he stuck out his tongue and then licked around the tip of my nipple. He knew just how to tease me. I loved the feeling of his warm tongue against my breasts.

I loved it even more when he started suckling on them. At first, he was gentle. He carefully moved from one breast to the other, giving each some attention as he very slowly slid his fingers up and down the slit of my pussy.

The rougher he became with me, the rougher I became with him. I was gripping his cock tightly now as I ran my hand up and down his shaft as fast as I could go.

I felt that we were each playing the same game. We'd played it before. We were trying to drive the other one to sex first... We were seeing who could be more tempting.

We were both winning.

It was me who finally had to break. Everything he was doing to my body was simply too irresistible. The stimulation on my nipples in addition to the rubbing of my clit... If I waited any longer, I was going to come.

"You have to fuck me!" I pleaded.

He smiled to himself. I could see the smug satisfaction, knowing he had broken me first. Though, frankly, after all that I felt like we were both incredibly close to coming. I didn't see how it could be avoided. At least I didn't mind a quickie as much as I used to. Now that we were having sex multiple times a day, it didn't much matter if it was fast or slow. We had nobody to hide from any longer.

He pushed himself into me, and I gasped at the overwhelming sensation.

I knew that there was nobody else in the rooms around us, so I allowed myself to moan like I wanted to and he allowed himself to do the same. .

Holy hell, I found his grunting so hot. I clenched my pussy even tighter around his cock, hoping it would make him groan louder, and I stared up at him as he had to close his eyes in ecstasy.

I began to push myself onto him from underneath, rolling my hips into him. He responded by fucking me even harder, sensual mewls and moans purring louder from my lips.

His seduction was all-consuming, every nerve

he hit felt so intense. He filled me so completely, and I was overwhelmed by all the sensations.

As his movements became more rapid, as fast as he could go, I began to lose control.

"Holy shit, baby, holy shit!" I yelled out.

"Come for me, babe. Fucking come for me."

I couldn't have denied him if I'd wanted to. My orgasm was nearing whether I liked it or not.

He was close too. As his balls slapped against my ass, I could feel how tight they were. I knew his body by now, and by the look on his face I surmised he was about to blow his load.

I wanted him to. I wanted his seed inside me. I wanted him to put a baby in me.

"Fuck!" he yelled out as his orgasm exploded within me.

Watching him fill me with his seed pushed me over the edge, and I screamed out incoherent grunts as the pleasure rolled through my body. As usual, I was trembling from head to toe. Edward was the only man who had ever made me tremble, and yet he was able to do it every single time he claimed me.

He didn't pull out of me right away. Instead, he laid on top of me, his cock still inside me. He just gazed into my eyes, his lids heavy and lust-laden. It was oddly intimate, and we connected on a deeper level, sharing this moment together.

Eventually, of course, he had to pull out. I knew he was exhausted because I could see his arms shaking. I couldn't blame him, he'd put in a lot of work.

He laid down next to me, a smile on his face.

"Pretty good, if I do say so myself." I kissed his lips.

"I'd have to say the same," he agreed.

I looked up at the ceiling. "Man, it's going to be hard to will myself out of this bed and go to brunch now. I think I'd rather fall into a sex coma."

He laughed. "Well, we don't have much of a choice. My mother is waiting for us. And, of course, the kids would be sorely disappointed if you didn't show up as well."

I really had been enjoying this trip with the kids. I was so excited to have a trip with just Edward and me, but after discovering Abigail and Drew were on board as well, I realized that was far more perfect.

As much as I was marrying Edward, I was marrying his family too. I had to admit, that appealed to me greatly.

"For so long, I've wanted to be part of a big family," I whispered to Edward. "The feeling really intensified after my mom died and it became just me and my dad. You know how much I love my father, but it's different—not having the nurturing comfort of a mother-figure in your life. We were suddenly such a small family, and it broke my heart. It made me even more obsessed with losing him because he was all I had. So, I realize how fortunate I am to be marrying you because I feel like my family has grown."

"It has," Edward assured me. "Even before the wedding, you are part of this family. The kids love you, my mother loves you. You could not be better suited to be in this family."

I grinned. "You really think so?"

"I know so. To me, you're already family."

I felt the same way about him. I wasn't sure yet when or where we'd be married and, frankly, it didn't matter to me. I'd marry him this moment if I could. To me, we were already committed for life. He was already kin. No ceremony could intensify this bond to me.

"Speaking of family…" Edward drifted off.

"What?" I asked.

He put his hand on my stomach. "Think we've put a baby in here yet?"

I laughed. "Uh, I think that would be pretty incredible, getting a baby on the first try."

"You're probably right," he sighed, "but a man can dream."

I was fairly surprised to hear this. "You really are ready for kids that soon?"

"You know, if you would have asked me a month ago, I would have said kids were a long way off for me. Now? Yeah, I could have kids now. I am ready to settle down. I see you with Abigail and Drew and I imagine you to be such an amazing Mum… It's hard to hold myself back."

"If I got pregnant now, wouldn't it be quite scandalous?"

He scoffed, "Maggie, I couldn't care less about scandal. If our most recent situation has taught me anything, it's that I don't care what goes on in the media with you by my side. Let them say what they're going to say. They've already fabricated a whole bunch of junk about how I've taken advantage of you. That doesn't make it true. They couldn't taint the blessing of a child if they tried... Not for me."

Fortunately, though, those nasty rumors about him taking advantage of me had mostly subsided. His press conference seemed to shut people up. I no longer worked for the royals and yet I was still choosing to date Edward of my own volition. That should be a sign I wasn't simply pressured into it.

"Well, then, I suppose even if we didn't get a baby yet, we'll keep trying." I kissed him gently.

He rubbed his hand down my back.

"Whenever it happens, I know that you're going to make an absolutely amazing mother," he said softly. "I cannot wait to bear witness to it."

This touched my heart.

"I am so lucky to have found you," I whispered against his lips.

"No, pretty sure it's me who is the incredibly lucky one."

Honestly, we were both incredibly lucky. Because finding a love like this—that doesn't happen every day. I would know, I'd lived much of my life as a single woman. I never even thought I was missing out on anything.

Now I realize that I was missing out on a lot. Edward brought a love into my life that felt so real and so complete... My life would never be the same and that was for the better.

"Come on," he took my hand, "we should be off before my mother gets too frustrated. As much as I'd like to spend the day with you, best we keep you on good terms with her."

"Agreed," I stood behind him and began to get dressed.

Though it may sound ridiculous, I had the faintest feeling that perhaps this had worked. Perhaps there was a baby growing inside me as we spoke. Maybe we'd soon be parents.

I was delighted by the thought.

MCKENNA JAMES

Epilogue

Maggie

Six years later

"And what color are the roses, Prince Heath?" I asked my five-year-old son.

"They're red, Mum! But the daffodils are yellow like the sun!" He planted his face in the flower and inhaled deep. "I love the smell of flowers, Mum. They smell pretty like you!"

"Thank you, sweet boy. Do you know why the flowers smell so lovely?"

"YES! To attract the bees with their pollen," he stated proudly. As much as I loved working outside when I was tutoring Princess Abigail and Prince Drew all those years ago, not much had changed since in that regard. Since Prince Heath was big enough to walk and talk, we'd take strolls through the courtyard and garden, and I'd teach him everything from the colors, shapes, and sizes to bits of Science, Spelling, and even Math. At five-years-old, his intelligence is flourishing.

"Very well, my sweet prince. Now, if you'd like to play for a few minutes, you may do so while Mum rests." Prince Heath took the small truck I handed him in reward for being so well behaved today and knelt to the ground, pushing it along the cobblestone. I sat back in the rocker Prince Edward had placed among the garden for me, so I could sit comfortably while teaching Heath.

My feet were so swollen, and the pain in my lower back was far worse than it was when I was carrying Heath. Yes, we are expecting our second child, another son would be arriving any day now. Edward had encouraged me to stay off my feet as much as possible, though I preferred to stay busy with Heath as I was sure once the baby arrived there would be minor jealously.

Heath was certainly a mum's boy, stuck right to my hip day and night. I was quite nervous to see how he'd adapt to life as a big brother because Edward was already talking about baby number three. He wanted a daughter, and who was I to deny that to him? After all, it was so much fun trying to make babies. My only stipulation was that we wait until the new baby was at least nine-ten months old before we start trying again.

Being a mum was all I'd hoped it would be, minus the struggles of my former life. Being the Princess of England certainly offered luxuries and prominence I'd never been afforded before falling love with Edward, and it was such a blessing to have no worries, troubles, or concerns over money. Over the last five years, I'd been heavily active among various charity organizations in England, helping single mothers and families. When I first told Edward I wanted to pay my good fortune forward to others, he asked how involved I would like to be—through donations or all in, hands-on working alongside the charity board and volunteers. I thought he knew the answer before he asked. No charity was too big or small to me. I did see a trend in the work I assisted in—there were mothers struggling to care for their families due to lack of education.

So, Edward and I founded the Royal University for Mums of England—a continuing education program that allowed mothers to get the training they needed for a career without being bombarded with the expenses of a true university. There were still certain fees they were responsible for, but we were able to help mothers all over our country through, donations and fundraisers, to continue their education and find jobs that would help them care and provide for their families without struggling. This also helped us build a future for our communities.

"Your Highness, are you finished with your tutoring for the day?" Millie asked as she entered the garden. After Prince Heath was born, Millie became my full-time nanny. I still had issues trusting her as a friend and confidant, and she still loved to gossip, but I kept her at arm's length. She did the job she was paid to do, and she did it very well. Heath loved her like family, and she always treated him with love and care. She'd been a Godsend in helping with Heath these last couple of weeks. I'm much more tired in the final days of my pregnancy than I remember from my first.

"Yes, Millie. Heath was very well behaved so I was just letting him play a bit before coming inside to get him cleaned up for dinner."

"Very well, Princess, I shall bring him inside now. Would you be joining us or do you prefer to spend more time in the garden?"

"I'll come inside shortly and maybe have a nap, Millie. I'm a bit tuckered out today. Have you heard from Edward?"

"Yes, Princess, he is expected to arrive momentarily." She quirks her brow in knowing, silently urging me to play into her conversation. "It would seem Prince Drew will be returning with him."

Now that, I was not expecting.

I quirked my brow, silently admonishing her. Millie's habit for gossip cost me my job as tutor all those years ago, and if not for Edward's kind soul, she'd been fired too for breach of confidentiality. Yet, the nerve of her to stand here and gossip about Prince Drew … It was unbecoming of her, and I'd have half the mind to report her to the Queen herself, but we had far more important issues of topic to be concerned with. Prince Drew was un-expectantly re-turning from boarding school during their spring break rather than going on the class trip as planned.

"Save it, Millie. I'll get the story when they both arrive."

"Yes, Your Highness." She curtsied with a nod.

"My sweet prince," I called to Heath.

"Yes, Mum?" He stood, truck in hand, and made his way to me.

"Millie will take you to clean up for dinner now, sweet boy."

"Five more minutes?"

"I'm afraid now, love. Mum will join you

312

shortly." I tweaked his nose, which made him laugh, then Millie took his hand and led him inside.

I rested my head against the rocker and rubbed my round tummy, humming quietly to the baby. The warm spring wind soothes me, and it wasn't until soft lips caressed my forehead did I realize I'd fallen asleep. My eyes flickered open to see Edward's smiling face looking back at me.

"Hello, Sleeping Beauty," he muttered.

"I didn't mean to fall to sleep," I replied on a yawn as I stretched my arms.

"How was your visit with Drew and the dean?"

"Not what we were hoping for actually. He's home now and may return to boarding school after spring break."

"What's the story there?

"Ah, you've had too much time with Millie, I see," he joked and pulled me up from the rocker. I jabbed in the side then took his hand.

"Not funny, Edward. You know I'm concerned

about Drew. I'd went along with you today if I'd felt like traveling. As much as I hate that he missed the trip to Greece, I am glad that he is home."

"Not my story to tell, lovely, and I doubt you'll get much of a response out of Drew. Besides, I only know what the dean eluded to me, and that wasn't much. Maybe there wasn't much to tell. Drew's locked down tight and close lipped about whatever is troubling him. I'm sure he'll figure it out on his own.

Obviously we were all concerned for him. Drew had always been vibrant and full of life, eager to learn and grow immensely. So when the headmaster reached out to Edward in regard to Drew's sudden withdraw, we knew we had to get down to the heart of the matter. Edward had made weekly trips to the school to check in on Drew, and each time he was dismissed as though there was no cause for concern.

As we entered the hall, Drew exited the library leaving the door open wide. The Queen sat with her face in her hands, obviously stressed beyond disbelief over Drew's situation.

I released Edward's hand and tried to hurry my steps, but my round belly had me wobbling unevenly rather than walking faster. "Don't you dare, Drew," I called ahead.

He swung around and stared me down, crossing his arms over his chest as he waited for me to catch up. "I'm in no mood for more sage advice, Maggie, really."

I realized as I approached him how much of a young man he'd grown into as I had to lean my head back to make eye contact. Standing at six-feet-one, it was safe to say he towered over me and still had room to grow.

"No lip, Drew. By the looks of your mother, I'd say the two of you have already minced words, but surely you wouldn't dare to be cruel and hurtful to a woman with child," I challenge him with my brow cocked.

He looks back toward Edward and then down to me, his shoulders slumping in defeat.

I took that as cue that I'd broke the barrier holding him in silence and walked ahead of him sure that he'd follow. Each step was painful, my back aching and throbbing under the weight of my heavy belly. I made it to the garden and sat in the rocker, taking a deep sigh to ease the pain.

Drew found his way toward me and sat on the bench next to me, looking around to make sure nobody was near to overhear our conversation.

"I can remember the first day I met you. You weren't happy to have a new tutor, and you doubted my abilities to teach you and Abigail. It's pitiful to admit, but I was intimidated by a twelve-year-old. Now look at you eighteen, a mirror image of Edward, minus the cocky attitude and flirtatious personality, and in your first year of university. You have an amazing life ahead of you as Prince, responsibilities that will weigh heavily on your shoulders, but if any one man in this family was destined to rule all of England, it was you, Prince Drew." He scrubbed his hand down his face and stared off into the distance, remaining silent.

"Drew, whatever it is, you can share with me, and it won't go any further. Promise."

"It's not what's wrong, Maggie, but what's right." He sighs, the defeat in his voice intense.

"I don't follow, Drew."

"You said it perfectly. I have my whole life ahead of me, as perfect as it may seem. It's anything but." He stared at me for a moment then asked, "What if I'm more like Edward than any of us realized?"

"What do you mean, Drew?"

"Flirtatious, irresponsible? Ready to escape the Royal life just for lo—"

I stared blankly as his words registered. The headmaster contacted Edward weeks ago concerned with Drew's sudden change in behavior. His grades were slipping, he'd secluded himself from friends, and his demeanor was no longer strong and confident, but cocky and dismissive. Edward and The Queen had tossed around ideas of possibly being bullied, though who would bully a royal; perhaps he'd been enticed with drugs? Suddenly the lightbulb of recognition flickered and I realized what the problem had been all along.

"What's her name?"

"Eliza Noble, and she's turned my world upside down.

Thank you so much for reading Royally Schooled. I hope you enjoyed Maggie and Edward's love story and if you did, I think you will love my next book Royal Academy. It's all about Drew (all grown up!) falling for a girl who appears wrong for him in every way, but she steals his heart anyway.

Order Royal Academy now so you don't miss it.

You don't have to wait for Royal Academy for more Royal Romance. You can read Bad Boy Prince FREE!

Download Bad Boy Prince now.

Also by Mckenna James

Royally Schooled

Royal Academy

About the Author

Mckenna James is the pen name for a collaborative writing duo who share an addiction to sweet tea and a love for wealthy, attractive men.

Since they don't know enough devastatingly handsome men with boatloads of cash to spare, they decided to create some. They specialize in fairytales for today's world featuring modern princes and heroines who speak their minds and carve out happily ever afters on their own terms.

Join her Reader group on Facebook.